SPECIAL MESSAGE TO READERS

This book is published under the auspices of

THE ULVERSCROFT FOUNDATION

(registered charity No. 264873 UK)

Established in 1972 to provide funds for research, diagnosis and treatment of eye diseases. Examples of contributions made are: —

A Children's Assessment Unit at Moorfield's Hospital, London.

•

Twin operating theatres at the Western Ophthalmic Hospital, London.

•

A Chair of Ophthalmology at the Royal Australian College of Ophthalmologists.

•

The Ulverscroft Children's Eye Unit at the Great Ormond Street Hospital For Sick Children, London.

You can help further the work of the Foundation by making a donation or leaving a legacy. Every contribution, no matter how small, is received with gratitude. Please write for details to:

THE ULVERSCROFT FOUNDATION,
The Green, Bradgate Road, Anstey,
Leicester LE7 7FU, England.
Telephone: (0116) 236 4325

In Australia write to:
THE ULVERSCROFT FOUNDATION,
c/o The Royal Australian and New Zealand College of Ophthalmologists,
94-98 Chalmers Street, Surry Hills,
N.S.W. 2010, Australia

PATHS OF FATE

When Sara decides to take on a lodger to solve her money worries, her unexpected choice of Walter as a housemate certainly makes life more interesting. But the situation becomes more complicated as her relationship with a charming newcomer at work develops. At the same time, her friend Tabitha is in danger of losing the man she loves. It seems as if their romantic problems can only end in heartbreak . . .

Books by Sheila Holroyd
in the Linford Romance Library:

ALL FOR LOVE
THE FACE IN THE MIRROR
DISTANT LOVE
FLIGHT TO FREEDOM
FALSE ENCHANTMENT
RELUCTANT LOVE
GREEK ADVENTURE
IN SEARCH OF THE TRUTH
ON TRIAL
ISLAND INTRIGUE
PURITAN BRIDE
KEEP ME FROM HARM
FAITHFUL TO A DREAM
A BAD BEGINNING
STAY WITH ME
HOME NO MORE
A HEART DIVIDED
MARRIED TO THE ENEMY
SUNLIT SUSPICION
DISTANT SUN

SHEILA HOLROYD

PATHS OF FATE

Complete and Unabridged

LINFORD
Leicester

First published in Great Britain in 2009

First Linford Edition
published 2010

British Library CIP Data

Holroyd, Sheila.
Paths of fate. - - (Linford romance library)
1. Single women- -Finance, Personal- -
Fiction. 2. Roommates- -Fiction.
3. Love stories. 4. Large type books.
I. Title II. Series
823.9'2–dc22

ISBN 978–1–44480–036–4

Published by
F. A. Thorpe (Publishing)
Anstey, Leicestershire

Set by Words & Graphics Ltd.
Anstey, Leicestershire
Printed and bound in Great Britain by
T. J. International Ltd., Padstow, Cornwall

This book is printed on acid-free paper

1

Sara Talbot went through all her calculations again with great care. Then she went through them again. At one moment she glared at her calculator and shook it, wondering if it was working properly. Finally she sighed, laid the sheets of paper on the table, and propped her chin on her hands. She had to accept the hard facts. Her mortgage payments were going to rise by one hundred and fifty pounds a month, and she couldn't afford to pay the extra money.

When she had bought her small terraced house in an outer suburb of London she had not expected this problem. Her mortgage was fixed at an acceptable level for two years and she had confidently expected to be able to cope with any rise without difficulty when that time was up.

Unfortunately she had not realised how much more expensive running her own house in London would be compared to living with her parents in a small Midlands town.

She was earning a fair salary as the personal assistant to the housing manager of the local council, but like everyone else at the minute, she was finding things very hard indeed.

What could she do? She certainly did not want to sell up and go back to her parents. They had predicted that she was taking on too much and there would be a definite air of 'we told you so' if she returned to them. The housing market was a little uncertain and it might be difficult to sell her house. She might even lose money on the deal.

Anyway, she enjoyed her job and living in her own house in London. Could she take on a second job to earn the extra money? She worked hard during the day and the idea of spending her precious evenings and weekends working at some part-time job did not attract her, even if she could find one.

Sara spent another hour trying to think of ways of saving money, with dismal results. She didn't run a car because she could walk to work in ten minutes, wasn't a shopaholic, and made her own sandwiches for lunch. Cancelling her daily paper would not save a hundred and fifty pounds a month.

In the end she went to bed early, telling herself she was saving on heating and light.

The next morning she confided her problems to her friend, Tabitha, during the morning tea break. Tabitha was blonde and bouncy but surprisingly shrewd when it came to money. She and her fiancé were planning to get married the following year and were saving hard. Now she nodded understandingly as Sara explained the situation.

'There are a few things you could do to raise cash. You could have a table at a car boot sale, for example. Bob and I raised just over a hundred pounds when we did that.'

'I haven't got many things I could sell. I was looking through the stuff in the spare bedroom, and I don't think people would be rushing to buy my junk,' sighed Sara. 'Anyway, I certainly haven't enough to do it more than once, and the trouble is that I need another one hundred and fifty pounds extra each month for the foreseeable future.'

Tabitha was sitting up with a gleam in her eye.

'That's it! That's the answer! You have a spare bedroom!'

Sara stared at her.

'What are you talking about?'

'You can take a lodger!' Tabitha stood up. 'It's time to get back to work, but I'll see you lunchtime to discuss it.'

The two girls met later on the park bench where they ate their sandwiches when the weather was suitable, though occasionally they had to raise their voices to make themselves heard when a plane flew low overhead on its way to the nearby international airport. Sara was looking mutinous.

'I've thought about it and I don't want to share my house with anyone,' she stated firmly. 'I bought it because I like doing what I want when I want. Anyway, just think of sharing a bathroom with a stranger!'

Tabitha looked at her patiently.

'Sara, either you share your bathroom or you lose your house. Which do you prefer?'

Sara shook her head, baffled.

'But think of all the other problems! How about cooking? Would a lodger want to use all my things, and suppose we wanted to cook at the same time?'

Tabitha patted her shoulder.

'You will have to set ground rules. Go home tonight and think of all the objections you can and we'll look at them tomorrow.'

'But I don't want a lodger!' Sara wailed.

'Of course you don't, but there is no alternative. Just think, Sara. A lodger will not only solve your mortgage problems but will even give you some spare money to play with.'

* * *

Sara's house was one of a terrace of small, plain dwellings originally built for workmen's families in the early twentieth century. The front door opened directly on to the street and there was a small paved yard at the back. Indoors the ground floor was now one reasonably sized room with a kitchen at the back. Upstairs there were two bedrooms and a tiny third bedroom had been converted into a bathroom.

That evening Sara stood contemplating the spare bedroom. There was a single bed, donated by her parents, on which her mother slept when she came to visit Sara. A tall cupboard could be described as a wardrobe, there was a cheap carpet on the floor, and a rather rickety table stood under the window.

Apart from these basic furnishings there were several cardboard boxes with miscellaneous contents which would have to be moved into Sara's room or thrown away. Presumably someone might find the rather dismal little room worth renting?

Sara went downstairs and made herself a coffee. A lodger would solve her financial problems and, after all, she did not have to take the first person to apply but could choose a suitable housemate. She had told Tabitha that she did not want to share her house with anyone, but she had to admit that there were evenings when she missed the circle of friends she had grown up with and felt just a little lonely. Perhaps she and a lodger could become friends.

Lunchtime the next day was spent poring over lists with Tabitha. It was agreed that light and heating would be included in the rent and that the lodger would be able to use Sara's appliances and kitchen equipment.

'You haven't got room for two sets of pans or two washing machines,' argued Tabitha. 'Now, I suggest you advertise in the local newspaper. Keep it short. You can discuss the details face to face.'

Sara nodded, and then hesitated.

'There's just one thing we haven't decided. How much am I going to ask?'

Tabitha looked thoughtful.

'Well, unfortunately this isn't a very glamorous area, and a lot of people can't stand all the planes flying over, so you can't ask too much.' She pondered a while and Sara waited anxiously.

'How about two hundred a month inclusive?' Tabitha said finally. 'You might be able to get more, but that spare room of yours isn't very big.'

'Two hundred would be plenty,' Sara said with relief. 'As you said, it will cover the extra mortgage payments and leave some over. That's all I want.'

On Friday of that week the local paper contained a brief advertisement: *Single room to let. £200 per calendar month*. That was all, apart from Sara's telephone number.

* * *

When Sara got home from work the telephone was ringing. A woman wanted to know the address of the house and how to get there. Sara gave detailed instructions and put the phone down. Immediately it started to ring again.

That evening she had at least twenty enquiries. Some callers decided they were not interested when they heard exactly where the house was, two hung up when they were told the rent was not negotiable, and she had to make it clear to others that she would only take one lodger, not two. However, five arranged to come to view the flat on the following day, Saturday, and Sara spent what was usually a relaxed Friday evening cleaning and tidying all through the house.

At nine-thirty precisely the next morning there was a knock on the door. Sara stood up, swallowed, tried to imagine herself as a landlady, and opened the front door.

A casually-dressed young man stood outside, his warm brown hair tousled by the wind.

'Yes?' Sara said coldly, wondering what he was selling but determined to get rid of him before the first would-be flatmate appeared.

'My name is Walter Crowther. My friend called you yesterday and made an appointment for me to see your room.'

Sara blinked. It had never occurred to her that a man might apply for the room, and she was sure that the friend had not made the situation clear when she called.

'I have got the right house, haven't I?' the young man said a little anxiously.

'Yes — yes, of course. Do come in.'

Sara stood aside. If she didn't really want to share her bathroom with another woman, she most certainly didn't want to share it with a strange man!

Well, she decided hurriedly, she would show him round, tell him she would let him know, and call him later to say he had been unsuccessful.

She briefly showed Mr Crowther the

living room and kitchen, then led him upstairs to the spare bedroom.

'I'm afraid it is rather small,' she said disparagingly, 'and rather bare.'

Mr Crowther walked in, thumped the bed, and glanced round.

'It would be adequate,' he announced.

'And rather noisy because of all the planes flying overhead.'

'Being near the airport would be an advantage as far as I am concerned.'

'I would require the first month's rent in advance.'

'No problem.'

Would nothing put him off?

'Well, I have several other people coming to view the room today. If you leave me your number, I'll call you when I have decided.'

He nodded and she led the way back down the stairs to the door, where he fumbled in his pocket for a piece of paper and scribbled his phone number on it.

'Here you are. I can give you references as well, if you like.'

He smiled appealingly, and Sara decided that he was rather a pleasant young man. She wouldn't have minded meeting him again, but not as a lodger. Unfortunately he showed no sign of wanting to meet her again except as a landlady, so she said firmly that she would let him know her decision and shut the door.

* * *

The remaining four applicants duly appeared, all of them female.

The first seemed to take it for granted that she would be accepted, threw herself casually into an armchair while assuring Sara that they would be great friends, picking up one of the ornaments on the mantelpiece and asked how much it was worth, then mentioned in passing that she would be bringing her cat with her.

Sara gritted her teeth and said she would let her know.

The next applicant had a perpetual

sniff and a braying laugh.

The next was very vague about where she worked and how long she would be staying in the area.

The last applicant was an elegant young woman who arrived in a smart little car, and was frowning deeply when Sara opened the door.

'Have you got a garage or a designated parking place?' she demanded without any preliminary greeting, and the frown became a scowl when Sara shook her head.

The young woman raised an eyebrow at the kitchen, explained that she didn't cook and demanded to know where the nearest good restaurants were, forcing Sara to admit that there were none in the immediate area.

The applicant shuddered at the sight of the spare room and put her hands over her ears as yet another jet plane screamed overhead.

'I'm afraid I can't consider this place,' she said coldly. 'I suppose someone may be desperate enough to rent it, but not me.'

The little car left swiftly and noisily, and Sara made herself some lunch and considered her options. Then she rang the second, third and fourth applicants and told them that unfortunately (for them) she had chosen someone else.

Then she dug out the scrap of paper and rang Walter Crowther.

'Does this mean I've got the room?' he demanded when she gave her name.

'Not yet, but it does mean that I am willing to consider you. Can you call round again this afternoon, about three o'clock?'

'I'll be there.'

Once again he was very punctual. Sara took him into the living room and, once they were seated, produced a sheet of questions which she had been busy working on. Her first question was about where he worked and what he did.

'I work in CGI — computer-generated imagery,' he told her.

'You mean you work in animated

films?' she asked, with vague images of children's cartoons filling her mind.

'Sometimes, but CGI involves a lot of other things as well. It can be used for special effects in otherwise live films, for advertisements, computer games or things such as flight simulators.'

'Which do you do?'

'I work for an agency who provide CGI services for a whole rang of things, but I have worked on several films. It is a cheap way of producing special effects.' He leant forward. 'I quite often have to travel to the people who want me to work for them. I frequently go to Europe and I've been to America more than once. That is why I am glad this flat is near the airport.'

Sara leant back in her chair. So he would be away quite often. That was an advantage.

'Even when I am here, I shall be working in my room more often than not,' Walter Crowther said, as if reading her thoughts. 'And I am house-trained. I can cook and I wash up afterwards.'

She looked back at her list of questions.

'Why do you want a room now? Where have you been living?'

'I have been living in a flat in Brighton. I've always worked with computers, but once I switched to computer-generated imagery I found I had to keep coming up to London or flying abroad, and Brighton just isn't convenient enough. I've been in London for the last ten days, sleeping on a friend's couch and looking for somewhere to live. It was his wife who rang you and made the appointment for me.'

Sara decided she had to be frank.

'Look, I need to let the room and in many ways it seems that you would be an ideal lodger. It's just that I expected to have a girl as my tenant.'

Walter grinned.

'I am a gentleman. You needn't be afraid I'd try and wander from my room.'

Sara blushed.

'If you tried you might get a nasty

shock! I'm no weakling! No, I was thinking of more mundane matters, such as sharing a bathroom.'

'I was brought up with three female cousins, all older than I am. I know all about sharing a bathroom with a load of females! Just leave me enough room for my razor and aftershave.'

Sara was tempted to offer him the room there and then, but before she could say anything more there was a loud noise from the front door where the knocker was being used very vigorously.

She opened the door and found herself facing a large, angry man with tattoos covering his bulging arm muscles and his shaven head. Behind him, urging him on, was the fourth applicant, the girl who had been so unsure about where she worked.

'So you decided my girlfriend wasn't good enough for you, did you?' the man snarled when he saw Sara. 'Well, think again. If she wants your miserable little room, you're going to let her have it!'

Sara stepped back, shaken and scared by this apparition, but before she could summon up a reply she was gently but firmly moved aside. Walter Crowther confronted the man. He looked relaxed, confident, and fairly contemptuous.

'Miss Talbot will decide who she wants as a tenant, and she has told your girlfriend she doesn't want her. Now go away, both of you.'

The man's face grew red and his eyes glittered with rage. He moved closer to Walter Crowther, trying to force him to step back and give him a chance to get in the house, but Walter stood his ground and even smiled a little. His arms hung loosely at his sides and he looked ready to spring into action. The bigger man halted, hesitated.

'Go on, Sid!' his girlfriend urged, sensing his uncertainty, and he swung towards her, as if looking for an easier target.

'This is all your fault!' he blurted. 'Why do I have to fight your battles?'

As the girl began to scream abuse at

the man, Walter stepped back and quietly shut the door and turned reassuringly to Sara who was hovering nervously near him.

'As soon as he stopped facing me he'd lost. He's backed down and he knows it. They'll go away now.'

Sara was looking at him wide-eyed.

'That was impressive!'

Walter grinned.

'It was bluff. I was trying to look like a martial arts expert and hoping he wouldn't take a swing at me anyway.'

She smiled back at him.

'Would you like to come into the kitchen? I'll make us a cup of coffee and then we can discuss the details of your tenancy.'

He looked at her with delight.

'You mean you'll rent me your room?'

'How could I reject you after you've saved me from that brute? Now, when would you like to move in?'

'Tomorrow?' Walter said hopefully. 'My friend's wife would really like to get her couch back.'

2

Sara was a little late for work on Monday, a fact that did not escape Tabitha. 'What's wrong? You look rather fraught. Have you spent the weekend interviewing possible lodgers?'

Sara grabbed a file her boss was demanding instantly and gave her friend a desperate look.

'I'll see you at lunchtime. I've got a lot to tell you.'

She reached the usual bench soon after one o'clock and collapsed on it with a sigh of relief.

'My boss has suddenly decided that everything is urgent. I've spent the morning digging out files and typing letters which all have to go out today.'

'Forget about work,' Tabitha ordered. 'Tell me about the room. Did anyone want to rent it?'

Sara groaned.

'Dozens of people, and most of them I wouldn't have let through the door!'

'But some must have been reasonable?'

'I interviewed five.'

'And?'

'And the successful applicant moved in yesterday.'

Tabitha's eyes grew round.

'Yesterday? Did you have time to check their references? Remember, we agreed you had to do that before you made a decision.'

Sara grimaced.

'I know, and that was all very well in theory, Tabitha, but in practice other things became more important. I have rented the room to the only person I liked.'

'What is her name? What is she like?'

Sara took a deep breath.

'His name is Walter Crowther. He is twenty-eight years old and he works in computer generated imagery.'

The last part was drowned by Tabitha's squeal.

'You've rented your room to a man!'

'Why not? There are plenty of bedsits with a mixture of men and women in one house.'

'A mixture — yes. People accept the idea of two or three women and the same number of men, for example. But you know very well, Sara Talbot, that if there is one man and one woman, people will assume they are a couple.'

'Well, in this case they will be wrong. Just listen to me.'

She told Tabitha about Saturday's events and how Walter had stood up to the belligerent boyfriend.

'So I felt he deserved a room,' she finished. 'Anyway, I like him. I think we can be friends.'

Tabitha was looking thoughtful. 'What is he like?'

'He's pleasant looking, though not handsome. He's got hazel eyes and brown hair. His eyes smile.'

'What is your mother going to say when she finds out that you have rented your spare room to a young man?'

Sara looked guilty.

'I'm not going to tell her, at least not straight away. Anyway, she won't be coming down for a visit for a couple of months and Walter might not even be here then. He's moved in on the understanding that he is on trial for a month. If either of us decide it is not what we want then he will leave.'

'Has he got a girlfriend?'

'I don't know. I didn't think to ask him. I liked his friends, though.'

* * *

Walter had arrived late on Sunday afternoon in a large battered car driven by Elaine, wife of Gordon Smith, who was Walter's friend and co-worker, and she had also overseen the efficient unloading of the half-dozen cardboard boxes that apparently contained all Walter's worldly goods.

It was Elaine who had recommended very firmly that the two women should relax with a cup of tea downstairs while

Walter and Gordon sorted out the installation of Walter's computer, which was obviously the most important item of his luggage.

'All they really have to do is plug the computer in and add a few cables and accessories,' she told Sara. 'However, they will then spend ages checking minor settings and connections, and if you aren't a computer buff it can drive you mad.'

She looked sideways at Sara, who was sitting bolt upright and listening to the noises from upstairs. 'He will be a good tenant, you know. He's quiet, tidy, and he will be away a lot.'

'But Walter said you wanted to get rid of him,' Sara said.

'Well, Gordon and I haven't been married long. We do need the place to ourselves, and ours is a rather small flat.' She looked round enviously. 'How did you manage to afford a house to yourself?'

'I was living with my parents in Leicester, but I wanted to get away and live my own life because my mother was still treating me like a teenager, telling me what I could and couldn't do.'

'Then my grandmother died and left me just enough for the deposit on this house. I convinced my parents that it was a great investment, and I suppose it will be if I can only pay the mortgage.'

Elaine groaned.

'I know! We keep looking for a house we can afford but the prices seem to rise faster than we can save.'

She stood up. 'Come on! Let's see if they have finished yet.'

The computer system still needed some fine tuning, but to mark the successful installation so far, Walter and Gordon drove off and returned with a lavish Indian takeaway for the four of them, together with a couple of bottles of wine.

'It's to celebrate my moving in,' Walter explained as he heated dishes and removed corks.

It was a very enjoyable meal, culminating with Gordon toasting the new lodger and his landlady, after which Gordon and Elaine departed, taking all the debris of the feast with them. Sara found Walter washing up the glasses and coffee cups.

'You haven't left me anything to do!'

'I'm trying to make a good first impression,' Walter told her, then grinned, holding out two wine glasses. 'However, there is still a bit of wine in that bottle over there. Divide it between us and we'll drink a final toast to each other.'

Afterwards he insisted that Sara should use the bathroom first before going to bed and when she woke up she found that he had already gone, leaving a note which said he would be back about six that evening. His coffee cup and plate were washed up and draining by the sink.

Usually Sara let her crockery pile up and did one lot of washing up in the evening. However, not wanting to appear untidier than her new lodger, she had washed up her own utensils after her breakfast, which meant she left the house just a little bit later and therefore arrived late for work.

Tabitha made Sara promise to keep her informed about the new tenant and then made her listen to ten minutes of complaints about the cost of wedding cakes and flowers. Sara, as she had done so often before, shook her head in bewilderment.

'Why do you want all these trimmings? Why don't you just go to a registry office, wear your best dress, and take a few friends for a meal afterwards?'

Tabitha, as she always did, accused Sara of having no sense of romance, and then it was time to get back to work.

The house was still empty when she got home and she took a frozen chicken curry out of the small fridge-freezer for her tea, reflecting that she and Walter would have to decide how to share the storage space between them.

Walter arrived half an hour later, a supermarket bag swinging from one arm, and swiftly inspected her kitchen equipment until he found her frying pan.

A little later they sat down to eat together at the kitchen table. As Sara started on her pile of microwaved white rice and a curry sauce containing unidentifiable lumps, Water slid a fluffy mushroom omelette on his plate and added some mixed salad. Sara felt a distinct pang of envy. Walter, on the other hand, eyed her plate suspiciously.

'Do you know,' he said conversationally, 'that the Indians don't have a curry sauce or curry powder? They mix individual spices until they have the flavour they want.'

Sara bit her tongue and did not reply, and after tea Walter pointed out that it was silly for them to wash up separately and insisted on doing everything himself, telling Sara she could do it the following day. Soon afterwards he went up to his room to finish arranging his possessions and perfecting his computer installation, only appearing briefly for a goodnight coffee.

Once again he left early the next morning, having washed up his breakfast crockery as well as the coffee cups Sara had left in the sink overnight.

That evening Sara had a baked potato topped with tinned tuna and mayonnaise. Walter grilled a fresh salmon cutlet and accompanied it with new potatoes.

He was upstairs when Sara did the washing up and when she had finished she sank down on the couch in front of the television, found a gentle romantic comedy to watch, and settled down for a comfortable evening. Just as the hero was pouring out his heart to the heroine in a moonlit garden, Sara realised that Walter was leaning over the back of the couch, scowling blackly at the television.

'What's the matter?' she asked, puzzled.

Walter pointed to the screen, where the hero was now kissing the heroine.

'Look at that! They aren't casting any shadows!'

Sara gazed in bewilderment.

'Should they be?'

'Of course! They've obviously filmed the scene in the studio and added the background later.'

He sat down on the couch beside Sara, arms folded and glaring at the television set. Ten minutes later, just as the hero's rival was trying to seduce the heroine, Sara jumped at a sudden howl.

'Just look at that dress! There should be far more folds and creases!'

Sara pressed the mute button on the remote control and turned to him.

'I don't care if her dress is too tidy or there aren't enough shadows! I am trying to follow the story. Will you please keep quiet!'

He gave her a startled glance, muttered an apology and then subsided into silence till the film had ended happily.

'I am sorry,' he said penitently. 'It's just that most of the people I know care about the special effects in films and get upset when they are not done properly.'

'But the story is the most important thing.'

'But how can you believe in the story if the setting isn't convincing?'

It was a good-natured wrangle, which ended without either of them being able to claim victory. In bed that night Sara reflected that although she could not hear Walter during the night as mercifully he did not appear to snore, she was somehow aware of his presence, and that was a comforting feeling.

She did complain to Tabitha as they prepared for work the next morning about her lodger's apparent desire for perfection, but her friend was not paying her full attention.

'He's just trying to impress you,' she said carelessly. 'Give him a couple of weeks and he'll be eating cold baked beans out of a tin and watching those sci-fi films you like so much without saying a word.' She checked her lipstick. 'Do I look neat, clean and hardworking?'

'What? Why?'

'Have you forgotten? The new manager is starting today. He'll be in charge of Environment, which is getting to be very important, and because the last secretary left, the new man will need a personal assistant and I'd love to get the promotion.'

'I had forgotten! Well, good luck! Does anyone know what he is like?'

'No. Apparently he was interviewed one evening, but one of the girls in Personnel has seen his file and says his record is very impressive. His name is George Sayers, and he's only thirty!'

'He's obviously a high-flier. Well, let me know what he is like.'

But Sara soon had a chance to inspect the newcomer herself when the General Manager decided to tour the various offices so that he could introduce Mr Sayers personally to the other managers.

Sara was busy with her boss, Mr Brown, trying to timetable the various committee meetings which seemed to take up so much time, when the

General Manager knocked firmly on the door, opened it without waiting for a response, and walked in followed by the new recruit, whom he introduced to Mr Brown before turning to Sara.

'And this is Miss Talbot — Sara — who Mr Brown is very lucky to have as his personal assistant. I know she is a great help to him. You'll be lucky if you get someone as good.'

'A good assistant is very important,' George Sayers agreed, smiling at Sara. She smiled back, feeling slightly dazed. Mr Sayers was bright, polite, and also very good-looking, with short blond hair and blue eyes, and his well-cut suit showed off a body that must have been the result of a lot of effort in the gym.

'I do my best,' Sara said feebly, and hurriedly released his hand as she realised that she was holding on to it for rather longer than was necessary.

After the exchange of a few more polite sentences the two visitors left. Mr Brown, who was middle-aged, short, plump and rumpled, sniffed disparagingly.

'Rather too smart for my liking. He's probably one of those young men who don't really care about the job they are doing because they are always aiming for the one higher up.'

'That's unfair!' Sara protested. 'Give him a chance to really show what he is like before you judge him.'

Mr Brown eyed her cynically.

'You haven't got a boyfriend at the moment, have you, Sara?'

She picked up an armful of files and swept out. He was obviously jealous of George Sayers' youth and good looks.

It was true, of course, that she hadn't got a boyfriend. Moving to London had cut her off from her familiar network of friends and acquaintances. She had gone out a few times with a man she had met at work, until she decided that he bored her stiff, and Tabitha had produced one or two acquaintances for Sara's consideration but without success.

Sara did not feel in urgent need of a boyfriend and was quite content to spend most of her evenings at home and wait for a suitable man to appear sometime. However, George Sayers was definitely very attractive and Tabitha would be very lucky if he picked her as his personal assistant.

But Tabitha was a little despondent at the end of the day.

'Apparently Mr Sayers has decided to wait a bit before he chooses a permanent assistant. He's going to have those who are eligible for the job working for him in turn, a week at a time, and then he'll choose.'

'That sounds very sensible.'

Tabitha screwed up her face.

'I suppose so. But it does mean that half-a-dozen of us are going to be competing against each other, and there is obviously going to be some ill-feeling.'

'The winner will be lucky. He's very charming.'

Her friend groaned.

'That is what everybody has been saying about him all day! Well, I'll do my best to get the job.'

'Bob might not like you working for Prince Charming.'

'He'll like the extra money.'

Sara's head was bowed thoughtfully as she walked home. She had been working for Mr Brown in the Housing Department since she came to London, and she respected him for his hard work and the way he really cared about the hundreds of people whose problems he had to solve. He was not a high-flier. He would be perfectly content to stay where he was for the rest of his career, secure in the knowledge that he was helping people and doing a good job, and he showed no desire to rise to a higher level of administration.

However, this meant that unless Sara looked for a job elsewhere she would also stay in Housing with him, and she did sometimes find it rather dull. Environment, however, was the current favourite of both national and local government. Anybody who succeeded in that department would be assured of a rosy future, and his assistant would benefit as well.

Sara shook her head. It was Tabitha who wanted, who needed, to be George Sayers' personal assistant. She herself should be grateful for the fact that she had a good, secure job, and a home of her own which she could now afford to pay for, thanks to Walter Crowther.

3

A fine rain was falling before she reached home and she fumbled for her door key feeling cold and depressed, but just inside the door she halted and sniffed the air. A warm, welcoming savoury aroma floated out of the kitchen to greet her.

Walter appeared, carrying a ladle.

'Come in. You're just in time to taste my soup.' Deftly he slipped off her damp coat and put it over the back of a chair, poured some creamy soup into a bowl and placed it on the table with a spoon. Sara tasted it gingerly, and then took another spoonful, then another.

'This is good!'

'Potato and leek,' he told her triumphantly. 'It's simple to make, but just right for a cold, wet day.'

'I've never met anyone who made their own soup. Do you do it often?'

'Just occasionally. It's a soothing activity and it seems to help me think. Today I was trying to solve a minor technical problem and getting nowhere, so I came home early and thought about it while I chopped and stirred. Now I think I've solved it.' He glanced at her plate. 'Have some more soup. There's plenty of it. I was going to have it for tea, with some bread.'

'I was going to have bacon sandwiches,' Sara said a little defensively, but his eyes lit up.

'Bacon sandwiches? Do you make the bacon really crispy?'

'Of course!'

'That settles it! Let's have my soup and your bacon sandwiches.'

When she had finished the meal Sara sat back with a satisfied sigh.

'Where did you learn to cook?' she enquired.

'Don't you mean 'why'? Neither of my parents could be bothered to cook and I had to learn out of self-preservation. Then later, when I started working, at first I found myself living in miserable little bedsits, so I used to make myself a good meal to cheer myself up. Anyway, I couldn't afford to eat out.' He gave a wicked grin. 'It helped my love life no end. Girls won't come round to see a man's etchings any more, but offer to cook them a special meal and it is a different story!'

'I can cook, too, you know,' Sara insisted. 'Only I need a special occasion to bring out the best in me.' A sudden thought occurred to her. 'In fact, I think it might be a good idea to have a dinner party soon — just a little one. I have met your friends and I'd like you to meet some of mine.'

'That sounds a good idea. Can I help with the cooking?'

'No! Though I reserve the right to call on your help if something goes wrong.'

Tabitha accepted Sarah's invitation without hesitation.

'Bob and I will love to come.'

'It won't be anything special,' Sara warned her.

'It doesn't matter. I shall enjoy having an excuse to dress up, and I am tired of spending my evenings watching television.'

'Why don't you and Bob treat yourselves occasionally?'

Tabitha shook her head forcefully.

'The price of an evening out would pay for the meals for three guests at the wedding.'

Sara forced herself to stay tactfully silent.

After some thought she had decided on avocado salad for the first course of the dinner party, followed by chicken casserole and then apple crumble with ice cream.

'I could make you an apple pie,' Walter offered.

'No!'

'Or a proper egg custard?'

'No!'

On the appointed date, Tabitha and Bob arrived carrying a present of a box of chocolates and were introduced to Walter. Sara was conscious of Tabitha examining him carefully and knew she would get her friend's honest opinion the next time she saw her.

The meal went well, with no unexpected culinary problems, and Sara began to relax. Walter tried to explain computer-generated graphics, with limited success.

'So it's like the old Disney cartoons,' Tabitha said, frowning.

'No. They were just a succession of drawings. We use the computer for a wide range of purposes,' Walter said patiently. He decided to change the subject.

'Sara said you two have been engaged for some time. When are you getting married?'

There was a significant silence, broken by Bob.

'That depends,' he said carefully, 'on how long it takes us to save up enough for Tabitha's ideal wedding. At our present rate, that means perhaps late next year.'

'But it will be worth the wait,' Tabitha

said hurriedly. 'It will be perfect. I will have a designer dress, all the flowers will be done professionally, and we will have the wedding breakfast at a really smart hotel.'

Walter was looking puzzled.

'But aren't all those things just trimmings? Why do you want an elaborate wedding?'

Tabitha's eyes twinkled.

'I want it because I was the third girl in a family of six children where money was always short. Most of my clothes were passed down by my elder sisters, and my mother made the rest. I want just one day of pure luxury, with the best of everything, so that I can remember it for the rest of my life.'

'What about you, Bob?'

'I want whatever will make Tabitha happy.'

They began to talk of something else, and inevitably the discussion turned to housing.

'We are lucky,' Bob said. 'My mother's house is quite roomy. I live there with her at present, and she has invited Tabitha and me to live there with her when we are married. I think it will work out quite well. Tabitha and I will be at work during the day and Mother will see to the shopping and housework. In the evenings she is often out because she goes ballroom dancing two or three evenings a week. As she says, we will be company for her at the weekends.'

Sara glanced sideways at Walter and found him staring hard at the table.

After the guests had gone, Walter insisted on washing up while Sara perched on the edge of the table nursing a glass of wine.

'Do you think their plans will work?' she asked Walter, and he shrugged.

'They may work for them. Personally, I think a newly-married couple need some space to themselves.'

'That's what worries me. I am very fond of both of them, but they are missing out on a lot of simple fun. Sometimes they seem almost middle-aged.'

'But they do love each other.'

His voice was wistful and she looked at him with sudden curiosity.

'You sound as if you envy them.'

'I do. I thought I'd found someone to love — someone who would love me in return. Then a few months ago she told me she had found someone else.' He gave a short laugh. 'Now, I'm not even sure I really loved her after all. I think I just wanted to be in love — and she was very beautiful.'

He wiped his hands and looked at Sara.

'Now it's your turn. Why have you got a lodger instead of a boyfriend or husband?'

'Oh, since I moved south I've been too busy with the house and my job to bother much about a social life. I've had boyfriends in the past, of course, but no-one I wanted to stay with for the rest of my life.'

'No one serious?'

'No one.'

'So you are completely fancy free?'

'Yes,' Sara said firmly, and then had a sudden vision of George Sayers holding her hand and smiling at her.

'You are blushing,' Walter said accusingly.

'Nonsense! I'm going to bed. Goodnight.'

It had been an enjoyable evening and the next day went well also. George Sayers appeared at her office doorway halfway through the morning.

'I'm afraid Mr Brown is out,' Sara told him, but he still came in, closing the door behind him.

'Actually, I came to see you. You may be in a different department, but I've been told you know best where all the information is kept.'

Flattered, she spent ten minutes explaining the intricacies of interdepartmental communication and where certain data banks were, and he thanked her afterwards with a smile that made her feel warm and slightly dizzy.

'I hope you don't mind helping me,' he murmured, and she shook her head vigorously.

'I am glad to be able to help.'

'Then perhaps I'll see you again.' He stopped smiling. 'Of course, Mr Brown might not like me taking up your time.'

'Then I won't tell him.'

They were fellow-conspirators, sharing a guilty laugh.

She told Tabitha, however, and her friend frowned.

'Why didn't he ask Joan Westly? She is acting as his secretary this week, and she could have helped him.' Her eyes widened. 'Perhaps he just wanted an excuse to see you!'

This possibility has already occurred to Sara, though she told Tabitha she was talking nonsense.

'Anyway, what did you think of Walter?' she asked.

'I liked him, and so did Bob,' Tabitha responded enthusiastically. 'I think you have been very lucky.'

'He did all the washing-up once you'd gone.'

'Then he's perfect!'

'Maybe too perfect,' Sara thought to

herself, though she did not say it aloud, but she thought it again when she got home and caught Walter busy cleaning the windows.

'Thank you. I was going to do that soon,' she said coldly, and he looked startled, catching the tone behind the words.

'I came home after lunch and I just thought I could help.'

Her lips tightened.

'This is my house. I'll look after it.'

He flushed.

'I am living here as well.'

She faced him angrily.

'Look, I know I'm not a perfect housekeeper. I don't mind if there is a little bit of dust. If you want perfection, go somewhere else.'

They glared at each other, and then Walter picked up the kettle.

'I'm going to make a pot of tea,' he said with teeth gritted. 'Why don't you go and change your clothes or something?'

Sara slammed the door behind her

on her way upstairs and immediately felt she was behaving childishly. When she came downstairs in casual clothes ten minutes later her temper had cooled. Walter poured the tea out.

'I'm sorry,' he said repentantly. 'It must have looked as if I was trying to take over the house.'

She managed a smile.

'I must be the only woman who would object to having the housework done for her.'

They drank their tea in silence, and then Sara sighed.

'I think the trouble is that my mother is a perfect housewife and I am reacting against all those years of never being allowed to make a mess or get dirty.'

'My parents were the opposite. They drifted from place to place and job to job. Eventually they left me with my aunt and her family and went to Thailand. They spent some time running a bar there till my father went off with some other woman. My mother arrived home one day, obviously didn't feel like looking after a young child, and soon disappeared again. The last time I heard from her she was somewhere in America.'

'My urge to have everything neat, tidy and clean seems to be a reaction against those disorganised years.' He grimaced. 'I know it can be irritating. To tell the truth, I think I was driving Elaine mad as well, and that was one reason she wanted me to move out.'

Sara shrugged.

'I expect we'll get used to each other. Now, there was some chicken left from last night. I think I'll warm that up and have it for tea.'

Walter's guilty look returned.

'Actually,' he said carefully. 'I did make a pie with the remains of the chicken and vegetables from yesterday. It seemed the obvious thing to do,' he added hurriedly.

Sara was torn between anger and laughter, and settled for laughter.

'Then tonight I wash up!' she told him.

The pie was ample for two and delicious. Herbs and spices had obviously been added to Sara's basic dish.

'Maybe a lodger who likes to cook and clean isn't a bad thing after all,' she conceded after she had cleared her plate.

'Try to think of me as a celebrity chef.'

Over the following weeks Sara and Walter gradually adjusted to each other, learning to share household tasks. She was surprised when he pointed out one day that he had been there a month.

'So what's the verdict?' he asked.

'What do you mean?'

'You said when I came that I was here on trial for a month. Can I stay?' Her eyes widened.

'Of course you can! Who else could I get who could cook like you?'

* * *

Tabitha approved of this decision.

'You have been lucky,' she said

warmly, 'but . . .'

'But what?'

'But I think it's a bit odd — Bob does too — that you don't seem to be aware of Walter as a man. After all, he is definitely attractive.'

Sara frowned. 'You're right. I hadn't thought of that.' She brooded for a while. 'I think it is because he doesn't care for me as a woman. We are just two friends sharing a house.'

'And anyway, your affections are otherwise engaged,' Tabitha said a little tartly.

'Nonsense!' Sara said indignantly.

'So all those visits from Mr George Sayers are just to do with work?'

'Of course!' Sara declared, but refused to meet her friend's eyes.

George Sayers did seem to call in her office for help and advice rather a lot, and he did seem, by a happy coincidence, to choose the times when Mr Brown was absent.

Increasingly, helping him involved doing some task for him. Sara was aware that he could have got help elsewhere, probably from his succession of secretaries, but did not point this out to him, hoping it was his way of establishing a friendship between them.

She seemed to be proved right when one day he put down the file he had been consulting and turned to her.

'Sara, you've helped me a lot, you know. Can I pay you back a little by taking you to lunch one day, or is there a boyfriend who would disapprove?'

'There's no boyfriend and I'll certainly come with you,' she responded gladly.

Apparently he had expected this answer because he had already booked a table for that Friday at a restaurant just far enough away so that they would be unlikely to meet any fellow-workers there.

Sara decided that Tabitha did not need to know the real reason why she could not see her that lunchtime and told her she had to go shopping. She dressed a little more smartly than usual, and met George at the restaurant, as both of them were aware that tongues would soon start wagging if they were seen leaving the office together.

The meal was unmemorable, but it was pleasant to relax and chat about something other than filing systems and sub-committees. They were both comparative newcomers to London and spent some time comparing their different reactions to the city.

'Mr Sayers,' she started at one point, but he shook his head.

'Mr Sayers is for the office. Please call me George.'

She had been thinking of him as George for some time, but it still gave her a thrill to be able to address him by that name.

George Sayers seemed keen to learn all about Sara.

'So you already have your own house?' he said, eyebrows raised. 'You must have a wealthy family!'

'No, just comfortable, but I was lucky enough to be left some money.

Unfortunately I've still got a large mortgage. In fact I recently took a lodger to help with the payments.'

'Do you get on well with her?'

Sara was about to explain that her lodger was actually a 'he', then thought again and just nodded. She remembered what Tabitha had said and realised that it was possible that George might be one of those who thought that a single man and a single woman living together could not be just good friends.

It was time to get back to the office. George frowned over the bill and checked every item.

'Let me pay for my lunch,' Sara said politely and was a little taken aback when he accepted the offer. It just shows he accepts you as an equal, she told herself, but it did niggle. After all, he had asked her out.

After that she had to hurry, and Mr Brown was already at work when Sara got back to her office and she apologised a little breathlessly.

'Don't worry,' he told her, eyeing her

elegant suit. 'You work hard enough for me when you are here. It's not as if you waste your time with people from other departments, is it?'

Sara gave him a startled look, her conscience suddenly uneasy over the time she spent helping George Sayers instead of doing her own work, but Mr Brown was frowning at a pile of correspondence and seemed unaware of having caused her any discomfort. Well, now she and George were meeting outside work, she could direct him to other people when he asked for help.

* * *

After the evening meal that night she was sitting on the couch, recalling all that had been said that lunchtime, wondering when or if George would ask her out again, when she looked up and saw Walter watching her.

'What?' she demanded, and he grinned.

'You're looking dewy-eyed and romantic. What happened today?'

She could feel herself blushing. 'Nothing important. I had lunch with — a friend. That's all.'

'And you are not going to tell me about this friend?'

He laughed as she shook her head. 'Well, good luck.'

On Monday she began to wonder whether good luck was with her or not. George appeared for a job for her that involved collating information and putting it on a spreadsheet.

'Your secretary could do this for you,' she said, mindful of her good resolution.

'But you will do it quicker and better.'

She nearly melted, but shook her head.

'I know Tabitha is your secretary for this week and she is good. Let her show you what she can do.'

For a moment she saw an expression of annoyance and irritation. Then the smile reappeared.

'You are kind, Sara. I know Tabitha is

your friend and you want to give her the chance of promotion. But is she really as good as you?'

In the end Sara agreed to do the work for him, but told herself it was for positively the last time.

To her surprise, Tabitha was not altogether happy to be working for George Sayers.

'I'm not sure I like him,' she informed Sara. 'He smiles a lot and says 'please' and 'thank you', but it all seems superficial. His eyes don't smile. He expects me to do an awful lot of work, including some that he should do himself, and then complains if there is the smallest mistake. The other secretaries don't like him either.'

Tabitha had obviously made some error and had resented having it pointed out to her, Sara thought. After all, George Sayers had said that not everybody was as efficient as she was.

4

Sara hung her head and felt thoroughly ashamed of herself. Mr Brown seemed disappointed and reproachful rather than angry, and that made her feel worse.

'I thought you got the message when I spoke to you the other day,' he said sadly.

He had come into her office and found her putting the finishing touches to George's spreadsheet. To make it worse, he was there to ask where a report was that she was supposed to have typed up for him. The notes for the report were lying neglected on her desk.

'I was going to do it next,' she assured him.

'You are my secretary and my work comes first. If some official wants you to do something for him then he should ask me. You know that.' He shrugged. 'Anyway, Mr Sayers has a perfectly good secretary of his own. Isn't it your friend, Tabitha, this week?'

Sara nodded miserably.

'So why did you do it? No — don't give me some excuse. I know the answer. Mr George Sayers is a good-looking and plausible young man. You wanted to please him. Well, he's obviously ambitious or he wouldn't have got where he is at his age, and from what I've seen of him he's very good at getting people to do what he wants. Don't let him use you, Sara.'

She didn't reply, torn between the desire to burst into tears and anger at his attitude to George Sayers. Mr Brown sighed.

'Get the report typed up by lunch-time and we'll say no more about it.'

Sara worked through her lunch hour but not only finished the report but also finished and printed out George's spreadsheet. She snatched five minutes to take it to his office, knowing Tabitha would be out for lunch, and she told him that she would not be able to do any more work for him, describing the scene with Mr Brown.

'You mean he begrudges you spending ten minutes to help a newcomer?' George said indignantly.

It had taken a lot more than ten minutes to do his spreadsheet, but Sara did not point this out. George gave her a rueful smile.

'I'm sorry I got you into trouble, Sara. In the future I won't give you any more documents to do.' The smile vanished and he looked anxious. 'Does this mean I can't ask you for any more information?'

'Certainly not. I'll always be ready to help you there if I can.'

The smile returned.

'After all, Housing and Environment have a lot in common,' he pointed out. 'Both departments are concerned with the quality of life. We should work together.'

'I agree,' Sara said enthusiastically,

and wasn't even disconcerted when she discovered that Tabitha had returned early and was at her desk in the outer office.

'Just something I had to bring over,' she said breezily, and left before her friend could ask any questions.

That evening she had gone about fifty yards from the offices when she heard rapid footsteps behind her and then George Sayers fell into step beside her.

'As I was the reason that Mr Brown was so unpleasant to you, I thought I should try to make it up to you,' he said cheerfully. 'How about coming for a drink with me?'

Sara hesitated, but decided that Mr Brown had no control over what she did after work.

'That sounds a very good idea,' she said gratefully. 'It's been a long, hard day.'

A few minutes later, nursing a cool glass of white wine, she tried to point out that Mr Brown had not actually been very unpleasant.

'After all, he was entitled to be annoyed. I was busy with your work when I should have been doing his report.'

George shook his head. 'But his report was done in time in the end. No, Sara, I'm afraid it may have been a touch of jealousy. Some of these managers who have been stuck in the same jobs for years tend to be envious of a younger man who is obviously going places.'

Sara leapt to her boss's defence. 'Mr Brown is very good at his job. He likes the work he does.'

'Then he's got no ambition,' George said dismissively.

They chatted idly about office gossip and office politics for half an hour, and then Sara glanced at her watch. George noticed this.

'Let me give you a lift to your house.'

Sara was just about to accept this offer when she remembered that Walter would probably be at home, and she wasn't ready to explain her male lodger to George just yet.

'Thank you, but the exercise does me good.'

'No, I insist. I've kept you late.'

In spite of her protestations he ushered her back to his car, parked near their workplace, checked her address with her, and drew up outside her house in five minutes.

'Thank you very much,' she told him, gathering up her handbag.

He had switched off the engine and was looking expectantly and she realised that he wanted her to ask him into her house, but she resolved that he was going to be disappointed.

'Thank you,' she said again, front door key at the ready.

A flash of annoyance crossed his handsome face before he accepted defeat, switched the engine on again and drove off.

'Who was that?' Walter asked when she let herself in and found him peering out of the front window.

'One of the managers who happened to be coming this way,' she said briefly.

'The one who makes you go all pink and starry-eyed?'

'Mind your own business!' she said furiously, but his laughter followed her.

If only she'd waited till she could find a suitable girl for a lodger!

* * *

Walter was already having a hasty breakfast when she came downstairs the following morning, still feeling a little annoyed with him.

'Hello and goodbye!' he said, reaching for his jacket. 'Gordon and I are working on something urgent for the next few days, so I shall be staying with him most of the time and I don't know when I'll see you.'

Well, that would be a relief! Once again she would have the house to herself. But after enjoying her solitude for a few days, Sara found that she was missing him.

She told herself that it was his cooking that she really missed, but gradually acknowledged that she had grown accustomed to the easy companionship which had grown between them.

She was amused at Tabitha and Bob's surprise that there was no hint of attraction between them. She and Walter only saw each other early in the morning when they were tousled and bleary-eyed, caring only about getting ready for work, and again at night when they were tired and had little energy for anything except eating and watching television. Romance was unlikely to grow in those conditions!

About nine o'clock one evening, after she hadn't seen Walter for some days, she was feeling definitely lonely and therefore came to her feet eagerly when there was a knock on the door.

Had Walter returned early and forgotten his key? But she was amazed to see that it was George Sayers who was standing outside, the smile on his face expressing his confidence that he would be warmly welcomed.

'Good evening,' he greeted her. 'May I come in this time?'

He was already stepping forward and she had no option but to stand aside and let him enter. Anyway, she had been wishing for company.

'I was working late tonight and I didn't feel like going home to a solitary supper, so I decided to come and see you. Here, I brought you a bottle of wine to make up for the lack of notice.'

Sara ushered him into the living room, and he glanced round before taking a seat.

'Isn't your lodger here?'

'No. My — er lodger had to go away for a few days.'

'Oh, yes. I remember Tabitha saying something about you being on your own for a few days.'

And wasn't that fortunate, she thought, as she opened the bottle and put it on a tray with two glasses, brought it back to the living room and put it on the coffee table. George poured a little into his glass, rolled it round his tongue, nodded, and then filled two glasses.

'Fruity,' he said approvingly. 'The man said it was a good wine.'

He was looking round the room again.

'This is a very pleasant little house,' he commented. 'Very well situated in some ways as well.'

'I like being able to walk to work,' Sara responded. 'I like the opportunity to get some exercise and fresh air before I start work.'

There was a brief silence while Sara wondered what to talk about. After all, she knew virtually nothing about him apart from brief details of his professional career and the little bit she had learnt from him over that lunch.

She need not have worried. George Sayers did the talking and it was all about work and their fellow workers. His descriptions were amusing, though touched with malice, and she found herself relaxing with nothing more to do than laugh at his comments and sip her wine.

He moved closer to her to refill her glass and did not move away again. Sara felt uneasy. She liked him, of course she did, but he was taking a little too much for granted.

'You said you hadn't eaten. Shall I make you a sandwich?' she offered.

'There's no hurry,' he responded, and his hand was sliding along the back of the couch behind her.

There was a sudden draught as the front door was opened and a thud as a holdall was dropped on the hall floor.

'Sara! I'm back!'

The living room door was flung open and Walter stood there, looking tired and unshaven but smiling. The smile vanished as he saw George, who stood up and faced him. Sara hurriedly rose as well, conscious of a feeling of relief.

'Walter, this is George Sayers. We work together. George, this is Walter Crowther. Walter is my lodger.' The men nodded at each other and Sara turned to Walter. 'I thought you were going to be away for another couple of days.'

'So did I, but the work went well so we finished early.'

'You didn't think of telephoning to let Sara know you were coming?' George asked coldly.

'Why should I? I live here.' He turned to Sara. 'I'll just change.'

When he had disappeared upstairs with his holdall, Sara found George looking at her accusingly.

'You never said your lodger was a man. In fact I have the distinct impression that I referred to your lodger as a girl and you didn't correct me.'

'Didn't I? I can't have heard you. Anyway, it isn't important, is it? Lots of men and women share accommodation nowadays. Walter is a friend.'

'If you say so.'

His tone was dubious and her anger flared. He had arrived unannounced and taken his welcome for granted, and now he was daring to doubt what she said!

'I do say so. Now, Walter will want to relax and have something to eat, so I think you had better go.'

She saw him to the door in silence. Once outside he summoned his charming smile again.

'Sara, perhaps I was a little hasty . . . '

'Goodnight,' Sara said, and shut the door firmly.

Walter came down in jeans and a woollen shirt to find her making coffee and sandwiches.

'I heard the front door. Has your visitor gone?'

'Yes,' Sara said tersely, and Walter grimaced.

'I am sorry I broke up your romantic evening. I suppose I should have called.'

Sara shrugged. 'It wouldn't have made any difference. I didn't know he was coming till an hour ago when he turned up on the doorstep with a bottle of wine.'

'Did he know you were supposed to be on your own?'

'Apparently Tabitha said something.'

Walter was looking grim. 'So he thought I would be away, and arrived without being invited, too late to take you out for a meal and clutching a bottle of cheap wine . . . '

'He said it was a good wine!'

'It's a half-price offer from the supermarket,' Walter said dismissively. 'It seems to me that it was just as well I came home early.'

'You sound like a Victorian father. I can look after myself.'

'Are you sorry I came home? Did you want him to stay?'

Sara thought for a while, and then shook her head. 'No. I'm not ready to spend an evening alone with him yet.'

'And you don't want to reach that stage, from what I saw of him.' Walter stretched out his legs and yawned.

'Still, I suppose we'd better draw up guidelines sometime about what to do if one of us does want to spend a romantic evening here without interruption.'

He saw Sara looking at him interrogatively and shook his head. 'No, I haven't acquired another girlfriend, but you never know when I may meet someone who fancies me.' He yawned again and scrambled to his feet. 'I'm exhausted. Time for bed.' He stretched out an arm and picked up George's bottle of wine. 'I'll use this up in a beef casserole. It's all it is good for.'

It was some time before Sara went to bed. She was too busy brooding on the evening. It was quite true, as she had told Walter, that she did not yet feel ready for a romantic evening with George, but that didn't mean she wouldn't want to eventually, and she was afraid that after that evening he might resolve he wanted nothing more to do with her. After all, she had virtually thrown him out!

On the other hand, it was up to her to decide how a relationship should progress. Walter was a friend, and her lodger, but that didn't mean he was entitled to tell her who was eligible and who wasn't. For a moment she found herself wondering whether Walter had felt jealous, then shook her head. He had never shown any sign of finding her attractive or tried to show himself off as a desirable partner.

No, the simple fact was that he had not, for the reasons he had given her, felt that George was good enough for her. Well, she would make up her own mind.

Sara looked at the time and decided she needed some sleep before she faced George the next day.

It was in fact mid-morning before she met him in a corridor. As she saw him coming towards her she tensed and tried to look business-like, increasing her speed as though she was on some urgent errand, but as they met he laid a hand on her arm, forcing her to stop.

'Sara! I hoped to see you. I wanted to have a word about last night.'

She faced him defiantly, but then

realised that he was looking apologetic.

'We parted badly, and it was my fault,' he said ruefully. 'I'm afraid I am a little old-fashioned and I was taken aback when I found that your house-mate was a man. Of course you were right, it doesn't mean anything nowa-days.'

'I should have told you about him, I suppose,' Sara conceded.

'His appearance would have been less of a shock. And, of course, I was very disappointed that our very pleasant evening together had been disrupted.'

He paused expectantly and Sara mumbled something to the effect that she had also been sorry at how the evening had ended.

'Then we are still friends!' George said warmly. 'We'll have to arrange to meet again, somewhere where we won't be interrupted.'

It was a pity that he said this just as one of the clerical assistants passed them, a girl who worked with Tabitha, and that lunchtime Sara was not surprised when Tabitha turned to her and demanded to know what was going on between Sara and George Sayers.

'Nothing!' was her immediate reply.

'Nothing? Then why are you going to meet him where nobody will interrupt you? Why are you doing work for him that he should ask his secretary to do? And Mary said she saw you in a bar with him the other evening. Come on, Sara. Tell me the truth.'

Sara shrugged, made a few false starts, and then produced a kind of confession.

'I like him. He's intelligent and good-looking and I think he likes me. When he wanted information and help I was glad to give it, not only because he was new and I wanted to help him, but because it did give me a chance to get to know him. He did buy me a drink, and I thought that was a nice way of showing his gratitude.'

'But Sara, if you had referred him back to me I could have given him the information and done the work. It might have helped me get a permanent secretarial post at a higher level, and you know how much I need the money!'

Sara felt herself redden with guilt. She should have thought about this.

'It was really my work as well,' she defended herself. 'After all, George pointed out that Housing and Environment do overlap.'

'Of course they do. And Mr Brown and the last head of Environment had a close working relationship. Why didn't George Sayers go to your boss?'

'He thinks that Mr Brown is jealous of him because George is younger and is obviously a high-flyer,' Sara muttered, and Tabitha almost exploded with exasperation.

'Sara Talbot! Don't be such an idiot! You know Mr Brown loves his job! You must know that when there have been vacancies for higher positions it has been suggested that he should apply, and he's said he didn't want to because he was happy where he was.'

Sara was silent, twisting her hands in her lap, until Tabitha heaved a sigh and put her arm round her friend.

'Men! They do make us do the most stupid things! I know George Sayers is quite attractive, but he's not all that special. Not many people really like him, for some reason. He still hasn't got a permanent secretary, and I think that is because at least two girls have turned the job down.'

'It's all right for you,' Sara said slowly. 'You've got Bob. I do get lonely sometimes, and the only place I can meet people is at work. All I do is come to work and then go back to the house. I feel dull and unexciting. It made me feel much better when George started showing an interest.'

'What about Walter?'

'As I've told you, he's a friend, that's all.'

'That's a pity. Bob and I really liked him.' She looked thoughtful. 'I suppose a few dates with George Sayers wouldn't do you any harm. It would build up your self-confidence, anyway. Meanwhile, I'll see if Bob has any friends he thinks you would like.'

'Don't you dare, Tabitha! I don't want you fixing me up with blind dates out of pity!'

Tabitha looked at her watch.

'Forget your love life! If we don't get back soon we will both be out of a job!'

5

It was two o'clock in the morning, the middle of Friday night, and somebody was apparently trying to break Sara's front door down. She could hear heavy thuds and raucous voices. Feeling rather scared, she huddled down in bed. Surely Walter could hear them too and would do something about them? Then she remembered that Walter wasn't there. He had told her that he would probably sleep at Gordon's that night. What could she do?

With an angry groan she realised that she had left her mobile phone in the kitchen, so she couldn't call the police. Then there was a louder crash and she could hear voices inside the house. Fear turned to anger. No one was going to break into her house and trash it if she could help it, and she switched on her bedside light, swung her legs out of bed and looked round. Her bedroom was pitifully short of possible weapons but she seized a large china model of a pig from her chest of drawers. That would have to do!

Sara opened her door and saw that the hall light was on and peering over the banisters she saw two figures in the hall. One was sitting, sprawled against the wall and the other was trying to help him stand. Incredulously, she recognised the would-be helper as Walter and the man on the floor as Gordon. She stormed down the stairs.

'What is going on? What are you two doing?'

Two faces turned towards her, both wearing broad, vague smiles.

'Sara!' Gordon exclaimed. 'The beautiful landlady!'

Walter tried to stand upright, with some difficulty.

'Sorry, we tried not to wake you up, but I couldn't find the keyhole.' He blinked. 'That's a very nice pig.'

'You are both drunk!' Sara realised,

feeling that she would have felt more dignified if she had been wearing more than an oversized T-shirt.

Gordon looked very hurt.

'Not drunk. Just celebrating.'

'Drunk,' Sara repeated firmly, and glared at Walter as he tried to speak. 'Dump Gordon on the couch and go to bed. I'll speak to you in the morning.'

She hastily retreated up to her room, very aware of her scanty attire. There were a few murmurs and some thumps, and then all went quiet. Indignantly she punched her pillow and finally fell into an uneasy sleep, only to wake up with a start wondering whether she had overslept before she remembered that it was Saturday.

There was no sign of life as she washed and dressed, but when she went downstairs there was a shapeless lump just visible on the couch which she presumed was Gordon, and she took a mean satisfaction in slamming the kitchen door and being rewarded with a feeble groan.

She had almost finished her breakfast when the door opened and Walter staggered in and sank into a chair. She saw that he was still in the clothes he had worn the previous night.

'Coffee — please!' he breathed.

She poured out a mug and was tempted to pour it over him, but finally pushed it towards him. A feeble hand grasped it and he drank it gratefully.

'More — and some orange juice!'

A few minutes later he was able to peer at her blearily.

'Where's Gordon?'

'On the couch.'

'Good. I thought I might have left him in the taxi.'

Walter rested his head on his hands and looked on the verge of falling asleep again, and Sara was just wondering whether to clash two sauce-pan lids together just for the pleasure of seeing his reaction when the telephone rang.

'Hi, this is Elaine,' said a carefully controlled voice. 'Do you happen to have any idea where Gordon is? I know he went out with Walter yesterday evening.'

'He is here, safe, on my couch and fast asleep. He and Walter appeared here very drunk in the middle of the night.'

There was a sharp intake of breath at the other end of the line.

'I'll be there in half an hour,' Elaine said in a tone that was half a threat and half a promise, and the telephone went dead.

Sara shook Walter. 'That was Elaine. We've got half an hour to get her husband ready for collection.'

He opened one eye, then another, and staggered to his feet as she bent over the couch and grasped his friend firmly. Finally there was a mild wail of protest, followed by a cry of pain, and Gordon could just about be described as conscious.

When Elaine arrived exactly thirty minutes later her husband was still far from his best, but his clothes had been straightened and his hair combed, and his eyes were open.

Elaine looked at him grimly.

'You'd better have a good reason for this,' she threatened, and then turned to Sara. 'I don't know where these two left our car, but I've got a taxi waiting outside. Help me get him into it and I'll leave you to find out from Walter what exactly they were up to.'

Each woman took Gordon by an arm and pulled him upright, then steered him to the front door. Sara waved the taxi off and then went back to Walter.

'Right, you've got half an hour to shower, shave and put some clean clothes on. Then you can give me an explanation.'

At least his eyes lit up at the sight of the fresh coffee and toast waiting for him when he came down later, though he still looked pale.

'So what is your excuse for last night?' Sara said coldly.

He mumbled something through a mouthful of toast.

'What? Repeat that.'

He swallowed the toast. 'It was Bobby,' he said. 'Bobby — the green panda.'

Sara stared at him, baffled. 'What panda?'

'Bobby, the green panda. Well, actually he's green and white, but the bits that are usually black are green.'

As she continued to glare at him, it seemed to dawn on him that a little more was needed, so he sighed deeply and began again.

'Gordon and I spend all our time helping to animate other people's ideas, and we decided we would try to come up with something of our own. People tend to see us as just technicians but we wanted to show we could be creative as well. So we came up with this idea for a cartoon figure.'

'Bobby, the green panda,' Sara said as light dawned.

'That's right! But then we had to get other people to think it was a good idea so they would give us the opportunity and facilities to develop it fully, and that has taken quite a time. Then, yesterday, an agent finally said that he thought Bobby had potential, and he's going to try to find an organisation that can use the figure of a green panda.'

'So we decided to celebrate with a drink, and then we had another while we tossed a few idea around, and suddenly it was after one o'clock and this place was nearest so we came here. I suppose from the way you are behaving that something happened when we got here and I apologise, though I can't remember what it was we did.'

'You nearly battered the door down,' Sara said bitterly. 'I thought you were burglars. You're going to have to apologise to the neighbours later.'

Walter groaned. The Harcourts on one side occasionally threw parties and would probably be understanding, but Mrs Drew, the elderly lady on the other side, had a very sharp tongue.

'I'll take them flowers.'

'Mrs Drew gets hayfever. Get her chocolates.'

Walter made his apologies, was forgiven by the Harcourts and lectured for ten minutes by Mrs Drew, and spent the rest of the weekend trying to atone for his behaviour by doing every odd little job he could find to do about the house. He also showed Sara sketches of Bobby, the green panda.

'He looks fun, as if he would make a good cuddly toy,' she observed.

'That could be one of his uses,' Walter agreed, looking proudly at his handiwork.

Sara also received a very contrite telephone call from Gordon. She had a mental picture of Elaine standing over him, making sure he said the right things, which cheered her up considerably.

'I still don't understand,' she told Walter, 'why people should regard the CGI people as technicians. According to you, quite often you are given just a rough sketch or even just a verbal description of what is wanted, and people like you and Gordon turn it into the finished picture. You are like artists painting a picture.'

Walter, back to normal now, nodded eagerly.

'That's how the best of us see ourselves. In a way, it is like mediaeval monks telling the painter they wanted a row of saints in the chapel. When he'd done the picture the painter got the credit, not the monks. However, nowadays it seems to be accepted that it is the original idea that counts above everything else. Anyway, if this agent can get us a good deal with someone, it could mean quite a lot of money, and that is always useful.'

'True!' Sara agreed. Ten minutes later a thought struck her. Would it be enough money for Walter to buy his own house? It was not a pleasant idea. She didn't want to go back to living on her own — at least, she didn't want to go back to living without Walter. Of course, it was because he was a good friend, and a good cook — that was all.

* * *

The next weekend Walter and Gordon were both in Italy with the aim of using their CGI skills to multiply the number of on-screen warriors in an epic, and Elaine called to ask if she could come to see Sara. She arrived in the Strachans' elderly car.

'It took Gordon ages to remember where he'd left it,' she informed Sara. 'It wasn't near the first bar they went to, not the last. In fact it was near a bank where they'd used the cash machine. And there was a fine for leaving it there overnight!'

'I'll bet you were glad when he remembered!'

'Indeed I was. It's old and rusty, but I couldn't get to work without it.'

'Maybe if the panda sells well you will be able to get a new one.'

Elaine laughed hollowly.

'If it sells, and if it brings in some real money. People can take out options for a fairly small amount on books, ideas, characters, but usually nothing ever comes of it.' She looked round wistfully. 'If we do get a reasonable amount of money I want to use it to buy a house. I do envy you having this. I am thoroughly tired of living in small, rented flats. I want a home of our own. I want a baby.'

She blinked and forced a smile. 'I can hope. Anyway, I came to see you to apologise for Gordon's behaviour last week. He very rarely drinks too much, and he felt so ill the next day that I don't think the incident will be repeated. So I've brought you some plants as a present. They are in the car boot.'

'Plants? What type?'

'Pelargoniums — we used to call them geraniums. They need very little care and are very tough, and they are nice bright colours. I know you've got a yard, not a garden, at the back, but they are in pots so you can put them anywhere.'

There were five potted plants. Three

had vivid red flowers while the remaining two had blossoms that were so dark they were nearly black. There was no doubt that they made the bare little back yard look much better.

'I grew them myself from cuttings and they are still a bit small but they will grow into quite big plants. I have the parent plants in pots in our flat. I watch all the gardening programmes on television and dream of having my own garden so that I can grow lots and lots of flowers and my own vegetables.'

A home, a garden and a baby. That was what most women wanted, but it seemed to be getting more and more difficult for them to get them. Sara thought of Tabitha, preparing to share a house with a woman who had lived there for thirty years and might tolerate a daughter-in-law living with her but was unlikely to regard her as having an equal share in the house.

'Gordon and Walter wanted to create an original character but it took them ages to think of Bobby. They kept asking me what I thought of their latest idea. I remember a pink chicken, a zebra, a blue horse and a rainbow-coloured spider. I didn't like any of them, but Bobby was quite appealing.'

The afternoon passed quickly and Sara was sorry when Elaine said she had to go. She had been missing the friends she grew up with, but as she watered the plant pots she felt she could count Elaine as a friend now.

* * *

George was surprisingly interested in the story of Gordon and Walter and their creation.

'A green panda? Yes, I think I could see that as a cartoon figure.'

They were having an after-work drink in the bar, the second time they had done so since George's encounter with Walter. George no longer asked her to do anything for him at work, so she was gratified to see these meetings as a sign that he liked her for herself and not just as a useful employee. True, they did talk about little but work, so she had been glad to introduce another topic of conversation.

'So he thinks it might be a nice little money-earner?' George continued.

Sara shrugged. 'He definitely thinks it could bring in some money.'

George smiled. 'Perhaps your friend, Walter, will decide to invest his profits in a house.'

She did not say that she had already wondered about that, but the fact that the idea had also struck George showed that it was indeed a probability.

'How would you feel about that?' George asked her.

'What do you mean?'

'Well, you seem to have got used to having him as a lodger. Would you miss him if he left?'

'Probably — for a while. But I could always get another lodger, possibly a girl this time.'

'Or you might already know someone who would like to move in with you.'

Sara's heart thumped. He was looking at her meaningfully. Could he possibly be hinting that he might be interested? She knew that he was renting a studio flat. Would he prefer the extra space of a house? One thing was for sure, she couldn't imagine George and herself sharing in the same easy friendly way that she and Walter did. She pushed her chair back.

'It's time I went.'

George looked impatient and a bit offended. He really did like to be in control!

'I thought we might talk some more.'

'Sorry,' said Sara, picking up her handbag. 'I have a lot to do tonight.'

She hurried out of the bar and realised that she felt she was escaping from him.

It was raining heavily, driving into her face as she walked home and she began to regret her haste. If they had left the bar together he would probably have offered to drive her home, and then she would not have got so unpleasantly wet. The house was going to be cold and dark, far from welcoming. She was hungry. Well, it would be a tin of soup and a sandwich, as she didn't feel like cooking.

But just as on another miserable evening there was a light shining through the curtains and a welcome aroma of spices when she opened the door. Walter appeared, tutted at her bedraggled appearance and helped her off with her coat.

'Sit down in front of the fire,' he instructed, before disappearing into the kitchen for a few seconds before returning with a cup of tea. 'Drink this and relax. Dinner will be ready in a quarter-of-an-hour.'

'I thought you weren't due back for another couple of days?'

'Everything went very smoothly. We finished early.' He put his own cup on a coffee table and sank down into an easy chair. 'I was glad to get home.'

Sara was smiling. 'I'm glad to see you home as well. I like being greeted with a warm drink and dinner already cooked.'

'No hurry. There's time to finish your tea. I thought you would be back earlier.'

'I went for a drink with a friend.'

'Tabitha?'

'No,' Sara said briefly, aware of his eyes on her and hoping she was not blushing. Walter said nothing, however, but just continued with his efficient work in the kitchen.

Summoned to the table, watching his quiet masculine competence as he moved about the kitchen, it occurred to Sara that their traditional roles had been reversed.

'What are you laughing at?' he enquired as he set out the food.

'I was just thinking that it used to be the woman who welcomed the man home with a drink and a meal.'

Walter raised a patronising eyebrow. 'May I point out that I am the dominant male, protecting and feeding the little woman?'

Later he asked her where she had got

the potted plants in the yard and she explained that Elaine had given them to her.

'It's a good idea,' he said approvingly. 'I was thinking that we could grow some climbers up the walls if we put them in big pots.'

As they sat companionably on the couch drinking their after-dinner coffee, it dawned on her that his gardening plans certainly did not sound as though he was thinking of leaving. She felt a surge of relief. She didn't want to have to adjust to living with somebody else.

6

'Mother! I didn't know you were coming! You should have given me a call. This is a surprise!'

'I know, dear, but then I thought I really should squeeze in a quick visit. Now, put the kettle on.'

Sara's mother, as overpowering as ever, swept into the house and sank on to the couch. Sara followed, torn between pleasure and dismay.

'Mum, I'm delighted to see you but I can't put you up, I'm afraid. I told you I had a lodger.'

Her mother waved a hand airily. 'Don't worry, my love. As it happens I'm staying in a four-star hotel near the centre of London. It's very comfortable, and much more convenient for the shops.' Sara busied herself getting tea and biscuits ready while her mother explained more fully.

'Joan Sudley, one of the Women's Institute members, had booked a weekend break with her sister, but at the last minute her sister had to back out because her husband is ill, so Joan asked me if I'd like to take her place. She's in Oxford Street now but I told her I couldn't come to London and not see you, so we are meeting this afternoon.' She looked round enquiringly. 'Where is your lodger? Don't tell me she has to work on Saturdays!'

Sara shook her head. 'Actually my lodger has gone to see a friend today and won't be back till late.'

'That's disappointing. Are the two of you getting on well together?'

'Very well.'

Sara, eager to steer her mother away from the subject of lodgers, started to ask how the rest of the family was getting on and what she was planning to do with the remainder of her weekend in London. The tactic seemed to work and they chatted happily for some time. Sara started to assemble a light lunch and her mother went up to the bathroom.

'Will salad be enough?' Sara enquired, busy washing lettuce as her mother came down the stairs. There was no reply and she looked up to see her mother holding aloft a razor — Walter's razor.

'You didn't tell me your lodger was a man,' Mrs Talbot said accusingly.

Sara thought desperately. 'Mother, you know I use a razor on my legs . . .'

'And aftershave as well?' her mother interrupted smoothly, and to Sara's amazement laughed indulgently. 'Come on, Sara. This is the twenty-first century. You're not the only girl living with her boyfriend.'

Sara was shocked. Mothers weren't supposed to be so broad-minded!

'He's called Walter and he is my lodger, but he is not my boyfriend. I didn't tell you about him in case you jumped to that conclusion.'

'It's all right, Sara. You don't have to pretend with me.'

'I'm not! Now sit down and listen.'

She told her mother the whole story — from Walter's first appearance, the way he had defended her against the angry boyfriend, what he did for a living and how well they got on together.

'So you see,' she finished, 'we are friends, good friends, but that is all.'

Her mother looked positively despondent, but then cheered up.

'But living together as you do, getting to know each other — there is a possibility that you might become more than friends.'

Sara gritted her teeth. 'Mother, he's seen me in the morning when I am definitely not at my best; he's seen me lolling around in my old dressing-gown when I have just washed my hair. I've seen him unshaven, tired and irritable. Romance will not bloom, believe me!'

Mrs Talbot gave a frustrated wail. 'And I thought that at last you were getting serious about someone! I want grandchildren while I can still enjoy them! Joan Sudley's already got three and she keeps talking about them.'

Sara thought how odd it was that she felt she should apologise to her mother for living with a man without being involved with him, and found herself offering a crumb of comfort.

'I'm not interested in Walter that way, but there is a man at work I'm seeing occasionally . . . '

Mrs Talbot perked up. 'What's he like?'

'Handsome, intelligent, charming . . . But it's early days yet. I don't want to say any more.'

'Still, it sounds promising.'

Mrs Talbot restored the razor to the bathroom and mother and daughter enjoyed lunch together before Mrs Talbot left to meet her friend and resume shopping. Sara had been pleased to see her but still felt mildly relieved when she left.

* * *

'She thought you and I were romantically involved!' she told Walter that evening.

'And what did you say?'

'I said there was no chance of that.'

Walter looked at her. 'Am I so unattractive?'

Thrown by this unexpected response, Sara tried to think of an acceptable answer.

'No, of course not. It's just that I thought we both accepted that we are good friends, that's all.'

Walter shrugged. 'You're right, of course.'

Soon afterwards he disappeared upstairs, claiming he had work to do.

Sara told George Sayers the story the next time they met for a drink, and was rewarded with a glinting smile.

'From what I saw of him, Walter is scarcely likely to make you fall in love with him.'

Then he leant forward earnestly. 'Forget him, Sara. I would like your help. You know the council is planning to acquire some sites to build houses and flats for sale to first-time buyers. Can you tell me which sites they are?'

Sara was taken aback. This plan was in its early stages and Mr Brown had sworn her to secrecy.

'I can't tell you, George.'

'Does that mean you don't know or you won't tell me?'

'I've been told to keep all the details secret.'

'But we are both working for the same council!'

'I still can't tell you. Ask Mr Brown.'

'What's the use of that? He won't tell me anything, and it is affecting my work! I'm disappointed in you, Sara.'

There was an awkward silence that ended when he banged his glass down on the table and informed Sara that he had to go. He left scarcely bothering to say goodbye.

Sara was sufficiently distressed to confide in Walter when she got home.

'He should know that I can't tell him anything about Housing which I have been told is confidential. If he and Mr Brown have a problem working together he should go to the General Manager.'

'He certainly shouldn't put you in the awkward position of choosing between him and your boss,' Walter agreed. 'If I were you I would forget him. Isn't this the man Tabitha hoped would choose her as his secretary?'

'Yes. And that's another thing. He finally appointed a girl as his secretary who everybody agrees was probably the worst of the bunch he had to choose from. She can type, but she hasn't a brain in her head.'

'Maybe he just wants someone who will do as she's told and not think for herself,' was Walter's comment.

Sara decided that next time George asked her out it would be best if she said that she couldn't come. In fact she didn't have to do this because there were no more invitations. George Sayers seemed to be avoiding her.

'I'm so glad I didn't get the job as his secretary after all,' Tabitha confided to Sara. 'The poor girl he did choose is in tears half the time. He's hardly ever there, he keeps missing meetings, and he snaps her head off if she says a word to him.'

'So you are free to concentrate on your wedding.'

'Yes,' said Tabitha unenthusiastically and Sara looked at her sharply.

'What's the matter? Are you and Bob having trouble?'

'Bob and I are all right, but I'm worried about his mother. I knew that moving in with her might mean difficulties, but now she seems to be seeing a lot of a man called Sam who she met at ballroom dancing. How do you treat your mother-in-law's boyfriend? It's embarrassing!'

'It's not a problem that often crops up on the problem pages! How old is she? In her early fifties? She's still young enough for romance.'

Tabitha groaned.

Any thoughts of George or Tabitha's problems were forgotten when Walter tore through the door that evening, already taking his jacket off.

'Sara! Have you got a posh dress?'

She stared at him. 'I have, as a matter of fact. It's short, silk and black, but what is it to do with you?'

'It means that if you can get yourself all dressed up and looking glamorous in forty-five minutes, I'll take you to a film premiere and on to a party.' He picked up a slice of bread and started biting into it. 'I claim first go at the bathroom. I need a shave and a shower while you sort out your clothes. Now get moving!'

Forty minutes later, when a taxi arrived to pick them up, they were admiring each other's appearance.

'I never knew you had a dinner jacket. I didn't think you even had a suit,' Sara said, taking in his immaculately formal appearance.

'Well, may I point out that this is the first time I've seen you at your best?' he returned. In the taxi he apologised for the short notice. 'Apparently I should have got the invitation a couple of weeks ago, but it was sent to the wrong studio. I'm pleased to receive it, anyway. It shows I'm getting known and my contribution to the film has been recognised.' He grinned. 'I worked on the big fight scene — lots of extra blood and the odd decapitated body.'

'How long will the party go on?' Sara enquired. 'Remember, I am working tomorrow.'

'Forget about that. Tonight will be worth being a bit sleepy-eyed tomorrow.'

The taxi edged through the crowd of fans outside the cinema. When it stopped Walter hurried round and opened the passenger door with a flourish.

'Welcome to the big time!' he announced.

Sara laughed excitedly, then looked down and saw to her amazement that she was standing on a red carpet that led up to the cinema entrance.

'We're going to walk along the red carpet!'

'And look who's just ahead of us!'

Standing a few yards ahead of them, smiling and waving to the ecstatic fans, were the male and female stars of the show. Sara gripped Walter's hand.

'Look! Look who it is!'

'I know,' he said, smiling down at her. 'Behave yourself and I may introduce them to you later.'

Meanwhile the television cameras focussed on the two stars were positioned in such a way that their picture also gave a clear view of Sara and Walter, hands entwined and smiling at each other. It just so happened that it was a slow night for news and the ten o'clock news editor filled in with coverage of the premiere which included a few seconds of that shot, which was therefore broadcast to the nation.

Blissfully unaware of the publicity awaiting them, Walter and Sara duly made their way along the carpet and were welcomed and escorted to their seats. Sara could not really have told anyone afterwards whether the film was good or not because she was too busy gazing around the audience, looking for famous faces.

Afterwards there was a jostle for limousines and taxis which duly delivered their passengers to a well-known nightclub. Spirits were high as everybody felt that the film had been well received. Sara was introduced to dozens of people and gave up any attempt to remember their names, and then she and Walter were greeted exuberantly by Gordon and Elaine.

'It's a glamorous do,' Elaine commented as she looked around, and then her eyes lit up. 'Food is being served. Gordon — Walter — go and do your duty!'

As the two men departed obediently Elaine located a small vacant table, appropriated four chairs, and sank down gratefully.

'Now I can slip my shoes off. I knew the heels were too high.' She turned to Sara. 'Is everything going well for you? Gordon said Walter had mentioned something about boyfriend trouble.'

Sara shook her head vigorously. 'It wasn't a boyfriend, just someone I thought might possibly become a boyfriend. Anyway, we aren't seeing each other any more.'

Before there could be any more discussion, Walter and Gordon returned triumphantly carrying plates of exotic snacks. They had also acquired four glasses and two bottles of wine.

It was well after midnight when Walter and Sara finally got home and Sara fell into bed aware that she might not be at her best the following day. In fact she breakfasted on coffee and aspirins and just made it to work on time. Mr Brown, already at his desk, looked up in mock surprise when she entered his office.

'It's Miss Talbot, the television star.' She looked at him blankly and he laughed. 'I don't suppose you got home in time for the news last night. You were there, standing on the red carpet along with the film stars. Who were you with? You certainly looked very friendly!'

He was not the only person to have watched the news. There were comments from various people, including a warning from Tabitha.

'If your mother was watching, she'll be calling you tonight and she'll want to know everything!'

Sara held her head in her hands. Even if her mother hadn't been watching, some of her friends would have been, and they would certainly have passed on the information.

Later that day Mr Brown came out of his office, frowning. 'Sara, I've been trying to contact Mr Sayers in Environment. Apparently he arrived early but he isn't in his office and his secretary seems to be on the verge of hysterics. Can you see if you can locate him? It is urgent. He should have sent me the information I asked him for at least a week ago.'

Sara tried various people, but nobody knew where George Sayers was to be found. As she continued calling, it became clear that she was not the only one looking for him.

'The General Manager has said he wants to see him immediately,' one secretary told her. 'I think there's trouble brewing.'

Sara decided that she really needed another cup of coffee and set off for the canteen. Just as she was passing a storage room, however, the half-open door opened abruptly, her waist was seized, and she was almost dragged into the little room. George Sayers' grip on her tightened as he thrust the door shut.

'Sara! At last! I knew you would have to come this way eventually.'

His usual composure and charm had vanished. He was sweating and looked agitated. Sara pulled her wrist free and began to massage it.

'What on earth is the matter, George? Half the people in this building are looking for you, including the General Manager.'

'I know. Don't bother about them. Sara, you've got to tell me which sites the council is planning to buy.'

Exasperated, she shook her head. 'I told you I can't, so don't ask me again.'

This time he seized both wrists.

'You've got to!' he hissed, shaking her. 'I'll keep you here till you do.'

Sara, frightened, acted instinctively. She brought her knee up sharply, and as it connected forcefully with George Sayers he gave a yelp of pain and released her. In a second she twisted the door handle and escaped into the corridor and then fled back to her office where, to Mr Brown's horrified surprise, she threw her arms round his neck and burst into tears.

Gently he persuaded her to release him, guided her to a chair and listened to the story of her encounter and inspected her bruised wrists. Grim-faced, he telephoned Security, then Tabitha, asking her to come and keep Sara company. Finally he marched out of the office, instructing Sara to wait for his return.

Sara sat shivering till Tabitha telephoned the canteen asking for coffee to be brought up and put a warm arm round her.

'I don't know what was the matter,'

Sara said shakily, 'but something is very wrong.'

Tabitha nodded.

'There are rumours going round the building. Somebody said it was a question of qualifications, somebody else said it was to do with references. Anyway, the General Manager is in a terrible temper.'

Mr Brown returned after half an hour. All he could tell them then was that George Sayers had been found, taken to the General Manager, and ten minutes later had been escorted from the premises and the attendants had been instructed that he was not to be readmitted. The building was buzzing with wild speculation until facts gradually emerged.

The General Manager had attended a conference where he had met his opposite number on the council where George Sayers had previously been employed. He had expressed his concern over Sayers' recent behaviour, which he thought surprising in view of the glowing reference he had been given, only to be told that in fact George Sayers had been given at best a lukewarm reference.

Further conversation had revealed that George Sayers had been asked to leave his previous employment. It had been discovered that he had lied about some of the qualifications he had claimed to have, and there were suspicions, though no proof, that he had been using his official position to get information which he had passed to property speculators in return for handsome payments. Within a few hours it had been discovered that the glowing reference had actually been forged by a girlfriend who worked in that General Manager's office.

Sara's General Manager had returned to work with the intention of challenging George Sayers immediately on these matters, but Sayers had been warned by the girlfriend.

'He is an inveterate gambler who is deeply in debt and desperate for cash.

Apparently he only came here today to make a last desperate attempt to get information from you, Sara, that he could sell to the speculators,' Mr Brown told her. He sat back and looked at her with concern. 'It has been a very upsetting experience for you. I know you liked him.'

Sara managed a smile. 'I liked him for a time, but I had gone off him long ago, so you needn't worry about my heart being broken. I'm just annoyed that I was taken in by him in the first place, and I am very glad that I didn't give him the information he wanted.'

'If you had, you'd be out of a job as well,' Mr Brown pointed out bluntly. 'That other poor girl who forged his reference has been sacked, of course. He seems to have specialised in charming women who could help him get what he wanted.'

7

Sara felt very sorry for herself all the way home. Not only had George Sayers been using her at work, but also she suspected that a man badly in need of money wouldn't have bothered with her at all if he hadn't known she owned her own house and therefore might have some money to spare. She wanted to be comforted but Walter was out and she had only just taken her coat off when the telephone rang. It was her mother.

'Sara, who was that man you were with last night, and if it was that lodger, Walter, how could you tell me you were just friends when you were holding on to each other and smiling like that? All my friends saw you. And how did you get invited to the premiere? Did you meet the stars?'

Patiently Sara explained how she and

Walter had come to be on the news, assured her mother yet again that she and Walter were not attracted to each other, and told her which personalities she had met at the after-screening party. It took some time and did not improve her mood. She had just, finally, put the kettle on when she heard the door open and Walter came in.

'You'll never guess what happened today!' she greeted him. 'George Sayers has . . . '

Walter interrupted her brusquely. 'I'm tired of hearing about that silly little man. I thought you'd had the sense to finish with him.' With that he continued on up to his room.

Sara was taken aback. She had never seen Walter in a bad mood before. She stirred the tea in the pot thoughtfully, wondering what was the matter.

There was a quiet cough. She turned and saw Walter looking sheepish and apologetic.

'I'm sorry,' he said penitently. 'I had something on my mind, but that was no excuse for being rude to you. What did you want to tell me?'

'Oh, nothing important. What is your problem?'

He laughed and rumpled his hair and gratefully accepted the cup of tea she poured for him.

'It isn't really a problem, more of a disappointment. You remember the green panda? Well, the agent has sold the rights to him.'

'But that's wonderful! Isn't it?'

'I suppose it is, really. It's just that Gordon and I had had this fantasy about someone making him the hero of a television series, and then a full-length film. There could have been models and stuffed toys, a computer game. We would have been rich.'

'And instead?'

Walter managed another laugh. 'The green panda is going to feature in the advertising campaign for a new cereal bar. He'll be on the packet and if there are television advertisements then probably Gordon and I will be asked to do them. It's just not quite what we dreamed of.'

'But presumably you will get paid?'

'Oh, yes. I don't know how much. The agent will be sending us the details soon.'

He sank down on a chair. 'Really we should be grateful that anyone wanted to use the panda, but there is a big difference between a television series and a television advertisement.'

He sat up, looking determined. 'It doesn't matter. Gordon and I promised each other we would celebrate if anyone bought the panda. Well, they have and we will. Can we have a party here, Sara?'

'Certainly we can,' she said warmly. 'Mrs Drew will never forgive me, of course.'

They agreed to hold the party on the following Saturday. Walter would make sure there was plenty of wine and beer, Sara would provide salads, and the local takeaways could provide pizza and kebabs.

'I'll get on to Gordon and we will work out who to invite.' He looked at Sara. 'Who do you want to ask?' Sara realised that he was thinking of George.

'I'd like to invite Tabitha and Bob,' Sara told him. 'And I'll invite the Harcourts so they can't complain about the noise. I can't think of anyone else I want to come.'

Walter looked relieved.

Over the next few days Walter saw to it that the kitchen began to fill up with boxes of wine and beer, with plenty of fruit juice for drivers. The freezer was packed with rolls and ice cream. Sara panicked at her lack of glasses but Walter informed her that he had arranged for a wine merchant to deliver several dozen on Saturday morning.

Tabitha was thrilled.

'I haven't been to a proper party for ages,' she confided. 'Are we supposed to bring anything?'

'I think Walter has made sure that we have everything we need,' Sara returned. 'However, if Mrs Drew starts banging on the wall I shall expect you to pacify her.'

Saturday was bright and warm, to Sara's relief. Walter, wearing jeans and a casual shirt with narrow blue and white stripes, looked at her with a smile when she came downstairs after she had changed ready for the party.

'You look pretty,' he said approvingly.

She twirled, sending the full skirt of her dress billowing out. 'That was the idea. I want to impress all these media people.'

He laughed, took her hand, and dropped a casual kiss on the top of her head. At that moment there was a knock on the door. The first guests had arrived.

'Let's party!' said Walter.

When the guests arrived they were able to spread out into the sunlit back yard as well as the house. Most of them knew each other and there was a buzz of conversation and laughter as well as the sound of music playing somewhere in the house. Sara glanced uneasily at the next-door house. Mrs Drew would not be happy.

Even as she thought this, there was a sharp rap on the door. Mrs Drew was on the doorstep, but dressed as if she was preparing to go out rather than make a complaint. She was wearing a hat and clutching her handbag. Instead of bursting into angry speech when she saw Sara, she stood waiting, finally saying, 'Well?'

While Sara hesitated Mrs Drew tutted impatiently.

'Let me in, girl. I am an invited guest. Your young man asked me.'

Suddenly Walter was by Sara's side with a welcoming smile, hands stretched out as if to greet the guest of honour.

'Come in, Mrs Drew. Would you like a glass of wine? There's someone I would like you to meet.'

He took Mrs Drew by the elbow and steered her through the crowd to a pleasant-looking middle-aged man and appeared to be introducing them. Minutes later Sara saw the man and Mrs

Drew in animated conversation and sighed with relief. Whatever Walter's plan, it seemed to be working. Mrs Drew was smiling!

Later she managed a quick word with Walter. 'What on earth did you do to Mrs Drew? She looks happy!'

Walter smiled smugly. 'Didn't you recognise the man? He plays John, the vicar, in Mrs Drew's favourite television soap. She is an addict. Every time it is on you can hear the theme music through our wall. He's been in the cast for five years so there is plenty for him to talk about.'

'But won't he be bored stiff?'

Walter gave a shout of laughter. 'Sara, he's only a minor character but she is hanging on his every word as though he were the hero. He's an actor with a big ego and he's loving it!'

It was a very successful evening. Sara met several friends of Walter who told her that he must bring her along the next time they were entertaining.

Mrs Drew was the first guest to leave,

and by then it was approaching midnight.

'Quite a pleasant evening,' Mrs Drew said a little grudgingly, but then smiled happily. 'John's promised to send me autographed photographs of all the cast.'

After midnight a few people with engagements the next day began to drift away, but there were still plenty of people there when Sara heard a sharp knock on the door. Wondering if anybody had come back to claim some forgotten possession, she opened it, but she had never seen the girl waiting outside before. She would have remembered her if she had.

The girl was tall and slim, her dark green dress cut to show off her figure, her glossy black hair was cut short, framing a pale face with enormous eyes and a full, pouting mouth. She was very beautiful.

For a moment the two girls looked at each other, and then the stranger lifted her wing-like black brows.

'Who are you?'

'I'm Sara Talbot.'

'Oh, of course. You must be the landlady,' and the girl calmly walked past Sara and into the living room where Walter was busy describing all the other peculiar creatures he and Gordon had thought of before settling on the green panda. His eyes widened and he stopped in mid-sentence when he saw the newcomer.

'Nicola!' he breathed.

Ignoring everybody else, the stranger walked up to him, put her arms round his neck to draw his face down to hers and kissed him full on the lips.

'Yes, it's Nicola. I'm back,' she said.

Gordon and Elaine came out of the kitchen just then, and when Gordon saw the new arrival he turned to his wife in puzzled amazement.

'I thought that was all over?' Sara heard him mutter.

'So did I,' Elaine said grimly, eyeing Nicola with open dislike.

After that the party lost its momentum. Walter seemed to have forgotten all about his guests. He was standing talking to the girl as though unaware that there was anyone else in the house. More people began to leave. In a short time only Sara, Gordon and Elaine, Walter and Nicola were left.

'I suppose we'd better start to clear up,' Elaine said loudly. 'Are you going to help, Walter?'

Her voice seemed to waken Walter from some spell and he looked round as if surprised to see the rooms empty.

'Are you going to wash up, Nicola?' Elaine continued challengingly, but the girl gave her a pitying smile.

'I'm afraid I've got to go now,' she said coolly, turning towards the door.

'I'll see you out,' Walter said, following her hastily.

Elaine looked after them with stormy eyes. 'How dare she! She hurt him so badly when she dumped him that I'm surprised she dared come anywhere near him again.'

'She probably heard that Walter has had a stroke of luck and wanted to find out if there was anything in it for her,' Gordon said cynically.

It was a good five minutes before Walter returned to face his friends' accusing eyes and when he did he grinned half-ashamedly.

'Sorry. We had things to discuss.'

'Really? Well forget about your old girlfriend, get a tray, and start looking for dirty plates and glasses,' Elaine ordered.

With the four of them working hard, the house was soon reasonably tidy and Gordon and Elaine left, promising to return the next day to help complete the job. Walter turned to Sara.

'I think it all went very well.'

'Indeed it did,' she said, yawning, but adding to herself, 'until that Nicola woman arrived.'

It had been a good party, she thought as she drifted off to sleep. Everybody had enjoyed themselves, even Mrs Drew.

She got up rather reluctantly the next morning and refused to look at what had to be done until she had had some coffee and toast. Then, instead of sinking down with the newspaper, she forced herself to tour the ground floor. In spite of last night's efforts there was still plenty to be tidied up and there were dirty glasses in many corners. She carried a trayful into the kitchen and ran hot water into the sink just as Walter came downstairs.

'Let me do that,' he exclaimed, but she shook her head.

'Have some coffee first. There will still be plenty left to do.'

Together they set about restoring the house to normal, putting the cushions which had been used as impromptu seats back on the chairs, and trying to remove the traces of wine and food which had been left on far too many surfaces. Walter talked cheerfully the whole time — about his friends, what they did, when he expected to see them next — about all of them except Nicola. He did not say a word about her.

Gordon and Elaine arrived about

eleven and the concerted efforts of the four had all traces of the party banished within a couple of hours. The two men put the boxes of glasses in Gordon's car and drove off to return them to the wine merchant while Elaine and Sara treated themselves to a cup of tea.

They chatted idly for a few minutes about the party, neither mentioning the late arrival, until Sara turned to her friend and demanded, 'Tell me about Nicola. Walter is keeping very quiet about her.'

Elaine snorted inelegantly. 'I didn't think Walter would tell you anything. Well, Nicola is one of those girls who believes she should be rich and famous, but doesn't see why she should actually have to do anything to achieve that happy state.'

'Nicola started out as a model and then found that to do that well involved hard work, so she decided to become a film star — note, not an actress — and hung around with anybody connected with films. That's how she met Walter

— at some studio when she had been hired as an extra. He fell for her, and you can see why. She is beautiful.'

'Then, after a few months, she wangled an introduction to a director and dropped Walter in favour of him.' She laughed. 'Unfortunately the director got tired of her very quickly, and the last I heard she was trying modelling again. Some acquaintance must have told her about Walter and the green panda, so she wouldn't have hesitated to gatecrash the party.'

'Walter certainly didn't mind,' Sara said unhappily, saw Elaine looking at her and added hurriedly, 'I like him. I don't want him to get hurt again.'

'Neither do I,' Elaine said sombrely. 'Unfortunately I doubt if he will take our advice. He's reached the age where he wants to fall in love and settle down for the rest of his life.'

They stayed silent, deep in their own thoughts, until Walter and Gordon returned with an Indian takeaway for lunch. They had also crammed into the back of the car several pots filled with plants.

'We took a detour via the garden centre and got a few things to add to the geraniums,' Walter explained. 'Now the house is in order we can see to the back yard.'

Pots were put down, moved, compared and watered.

'We will have a good display if they all grow,' Walter said hopefully.

'Otherwise you will have a fine collection of sticks,' Gordon said flatly. 'That rose needs to go where it will get more sun.'

'I don't care,' said Elaine, yawning widely. 'Take me home before I fall asleep.'

Once they had gone, Walter and Sara slumped into a pleasant stupor and both stumbled up to bed much earlier than usual.

Sara went to work on Monday expecting to enjoy a pleasant analysis of the party and the guests with Tabitha, but her friend, heavy-eyed, had little to say at lunchtime.

'What's the matter?' Sara said at last, mildly irritated. 'Didn't you hear what I said about Mrs Drew?'

Tabitha nodded. 'Yes. And I know what you mean about that girl, Nicola.'

'But you are just not interested!'

'It's not that.' Tabitha sat up, struggling for words. 'It's just that I can't forget what happened yesterday.' She paused unhappily. 'Bob and I always have Sunday lunch with his mother so I went round as usual. His mother was obviously bursting to tell us something but made us wait until after the meal. Then she told us that Sam, the man I told you about, had asked her to marry him and she had accepted!'

Sara waited but Tabitha did not say any more. 'So?' Sara prompted.

'So she said they plan to get married very soon and I don't know what effect this will have on our plans! His mother has invited him to Sunday lunch next week so that we can meet him and talk about the future. I'm worried. Bob and

I could have lived with his mother perfectly happily, but how will this Sam feel about us being in the same house?'

'If they both intend to be there. Where does he live now?'

'I'm not sure. Bob's mother said something about him living with his daughter.'

'Why not wait till you find out the facts and what they actually plan to do? Maybe he has his own house. Maybe Bob's mother will move in with him and give you her house!'

'That is not very likely,' Tabitha murmured dolefully.

Sara couldn't help thinking that Tabitha should be glad that her future mother-in-law had found new happiness and not be concerned solely with her own interests, but remained tactfully silent.

8

Walter was coming downstairs when Sara let herself in. His hair was still wet from a shower and he was wearing his best jacket.

'Going out?' she queried.

'Yes.' He hesitated. 'In fact I'm taking Nicola to dinner. You remember her, she came to the party.'

'I remember.'

Her voice must have shown her feelings for he followed her into the kitchen where he faced her with his hands dug into his pockets.

'It sounds as if Elaine told you about her and what happened between us in the past. Well, Elaine only knows one side of the story. Don't judge Nicola by what she says.'

'It's no concern of mine,' Sara said coldly, and his face grew bleak.

'No, it isn't. Anyway, I shall probably be back late.'

He left the room and she heard the front door open and shut behind him. Sara thumped her mug on the table with unnecessary force. That had been stupid of her! He wasn't likely to listen to any advice she might feel like giving if she antagonised him.

Sara stayed up later than usual, hoping to have a chance to repair the rift between them, but was finally driven to bed by the urge to sleep. In spite of his late return Walter had already left when she woke up the next morning. There was a note on the bread board saying that he would be away that night and possibly the following night as well. He was probably working with Gordon and sleeping at his flat, she told herself.

When she came home on the third day she nearly tripped over a flight bag in the hall. Walter came out of the kitchen with a sandwich in one hand and a mug of coffee in the other.

'Sara! I hoped to see you before I left.'

She slipped off her coat. 'You're leaving? For how long? Where are you going?'

'I'm going to New York for at least a month, possibly longer, but I'll let you know. You've got my email address as well as my mobile number, so you can contact me if you need me.' He nodded at an envelope on the table as he took another bite of the sandwich. 'There's a cheque for the month's rent there.'

Sara sank on to a chair. 'Rent? I'm not sure what you should pay if you're not going to be here.'

'I shall be coming back,' he said almost fiercely, and then managed a smile. 'This is my home, Sara.'

He seemed about to say more, but at that moment there was a knock at the door and he groaned.

'That will be the taxi for the airport. Look after yourself, and the plants.'

She followed him to the door and waved as the taxi drew away.

'Don't tell me your young man's leaving you!' It was Mrs Drew, standing in her doorway.

'Mr Crowther is simply going to America to work for a few weeks,' Sara said coldly, 'and he is not my young man.'

Mrs Drew sniffed. 'Well, you're living together, and if he isn't your young man then you are a fool!'

With that she shut her front door firmly, leaving Sara seething.

Work was no consolation. Tabitha was fretful, imagining all kinds of disasters for the coming Sunday lunch, and George Sayers' abrupt departure had left Environment in chaos and created difficulties for the other departments which formed the team. Sara was glad to get home on Friday and sink down with a consoling glass of wine, but her peace was disturbed by a telephone call from Elaine.

'Are you all right? You can come and stay with us whenever you like. A month is a long time to be by yourself.'

Sara laughed. 'Elaine, I was here by myself for two years before Walter moved in. I'll be perfectly all right.'

'Yes, but it's different when you've got used to living with someone. I miss Gordon like mad when he goes away for a night.'

Sara reflected that there was a difference between a husband and a lodger.

'Don't worry. I'll be fine. Was there anything else?'

There was a short pause before Elaine spoke again. 'Gordon went to the airport to give Walter some papers. Nicola was checking in for the same flight.'

Both women were silent. 'Let's hope she meets somebody really rich in New York and abandons Walter again,' Sara said at last with a touch of venom in her voice.

'I do hope so! Incidentally, talking of rich men, the agent will finally be letting us know in a few days how much Walter and Gordon will be getting for the rights to the green panda. Maybe it will be enough for a really good holiday.'

The call ended soon afterwards and Sara wandered out into the backyard. Some of the plants Walter had installed were already in flower and perfuming the air.

'Nasty Nicola may get Walter, but he gave you to me,' Sara told them as she watered them. She thought of Walter and Nicola together in New York and hoped desperately that Nicola would not hurt him.

She thought of Tabitha also during the weekend and wished her well, but one look at her friend on Monday showed her wish had not been granted.

'Sam's going to move in with Bob's mother! Apparently he lives in a kind of granny flat in his daughter's house at the moment, and she's delighted he's moving out because then her teenage son can move into the granny flat.'

'But did you like him? Do you think you could live with him?'

'He's all right, I suppose. Bob keeps saying that Sam and his mother will be happy together. He's supposed to be thinking of us, not them!'

'Let me put it another way, Tabitha. How do you think Sam will feel about living with you and Bob?'

'I'm not sure. He said something about being sure we could all get along together 'until you get your own place' so he obviously doesn't see us living there for ever.' Her face crumpled and Sara was afraid she was going to cry. 'He's upsetting all my plans! Just when I thought I'd got everything organised!'

'When are you seeing him again?'

'Next Sunday. He'll be coming to every Sunday lunch now. Bob's mother says he is part of the family.'

'Perhaps things will sort themselves out.'

But the following Monday morning Tabitha brought some documents to Mr Brown's office and when he asked her a simple, innocuous question she burst into tears. Mr Brown handed her over to Sara and fled. Sara fussed over her with tissues and coffee and finally decided she had recovered enough to be asked questions.

'What's caused this, Tabitha? Was is Sam yesterday?'

The tears returned, harder than ever, but at length Sara managed to extract the information that Sam was not directly responsible.

'But he and Bob's mother said they were planning to get married as soon as possible, no fuss, just ten minutes in a registry office with Bob and me, because they want to be together as soon as they can. Afterwards Bob and I started arguing because he said we should do the same instead of waiting till we can afford a big wedding.'

'He said the wedding seemed more important to me than being married to him! The row got worse and in the end I told him I was glad we had waited because I'd decided I didn't want to marry him after all. I didn't mean it, I was just angry, but once I'd said it I couldn't take it back. In the end . . . ' She held up her left hand and Sara was shocked to see that the engagement ring Tabitha had worn so proudly for so long was gone. Only a circle of pale skin showed where it had been.

'He'll realise you didn't mean it,' Sara tried to comfort her friend.

'He didn't call last night.'

'Give him time.'

Each day that week Sara waited to hear that the couple were reconciled, but each day Tabitha had to say that Bob had not contacted her.

'Why don't you call him?' she suggested, but Tabitha tossed her head.

'Go crawling to him and ask him to take me back? I've more pride!'

'Perhaps that is just how Bob feels.'

'Well, I'm not going to make the first move.'

Sara longed to tell Tabitha to stop being stupid, but she still had some sympathy for her. Her friend really loved Bob, she knew, but the big wedding which had dominated Tabitha's thoughts for so long was to have been a symbol marking the final end of her early poverty-stricken years. She had become obsessed with it and it must have been very painful to have her dream destroyed.

After a week of being supportive, Sara decided to treat herself and go shopping. She spent a happy couple of hours in Oxford Street, buying several little treats, and then decided to go and peer in the windows of Piccadilly's exclusive and expensive stores. She was gazing at an exquisite dress in one window when the shop door opened abruptly and a young woman strode out, brushing past Sara, who looked at her, suddenly realised she recognised her, and gasped, 'Nicola!'

At the sound of her name the girl turned, eyebrows lifted.

'Yes? Do I know you?'

'You probably don't remember me,' Sara stammered, completely thrown by the sight of the girl who she had believed to be with Walter in New York. 'You came to a party at my house. Walter Crowther was there.'

At Walter's name Nicola frowned.

'I remember.'

'Someone told me you were in New York with him.'

Nicola flushed angrily. 'No chance! I went to that party to give him a second chance. Do you know, he took me out to dinner a few days later and then at the end of the meal he told me he'd decided he didn't want to see me any more and sent me home in a taxi!'

'But you went to America with him!'

'I went on the same plane!' Nicola said angrily. 'I was going to America to do some modelling. Walter was in Business Class, and as I was in Economy I thought the least he could do was get me an upgrade, but he wouldn't help. That was the last time I saw him and if you are still his landlady you can tell him that I don't want to see him again!'

She turned on her high heels and strode away, leaving Sara staring after her. Two or three times on her way home Sara saw people glancing at her curiously and realised they must be wondering why she was smiling so broadly. Walter was safe from Nicola!

He had realised what a little gold digger she was and got rid of her!

There was a large white envelope addressed to Walter on the doormat when she got home and she wondered what to do with it. So far during his absence all the post which had come for him had clearly been junk mail, but this letter had a name and return address which she did not recognise and it might be important.

Should she send it on to him? She decided to email him and tell him about it. So far she had refrained from communication with him because she had imagined Nicola reading anything she sent, laughing at any friendly touches, but now she knew there was no danger of that.

At that moment the telephone rang. It was Elaine, almost incoherent with excitement.

'Sara, has Walter got a letter, a big white one?'

'Yes, I was wondering what to do with it.'

'You don't have to do anything. Just keep it safe. Gordon got the same letter and he's already contacted Walter. Isn't it marvellous?'

'What?'

'What the letter says!'

'What does the letter say?'

'Oh!' There was a long pause as though Elaine had taken a deep breath. Then the words poured out. 'It's from the agent — the panda agent! The firm are going to pay Gordon and Walter to do television advertisements as well as buying the rights! And they are going to pay them loads of money — enough for a deposit on a house!'

'But that's wonderful!'

'Isn't it? I've already been to the local estate agents and got details of loads of houses and Gordon is going to see about a mortgage on Monday.' Her voice grew lower. 'I just hope Walter has enough sense not to tell Nicola how much he is being paid or she won't rest till she's got her hands on it.'

'That's all right. She's in England

and she doesn't want to see him any more.'

Rapidly Sara described her unexpected encounter with Nicola and heard Elaine's gusty sigh of relief.

'Two bits of very good news in one day! I'll call you later this week. We start house hunting tomorrow!'

Sara put the telephone down slowly. So Walter was going to get a lot of money — enough for a deposit on a house. Perhaps he would change his mind about regarding Sara's house as his home, especially after their angry words about Nicola. She had been sure that he had gone out that night hoping that Nicola had come back into his life to stay.

What had changed his mind and made him send her away? The question niggled at her while she did various household chores and while she prepared her tea. Since Walter had gone she had reverted to her old habits and tea was a ready meal heated in the microwave.

She was halfway through it when the telephone rang again. This time it was Tabitha, apparently unable to get through the weekend without a sympathetic ear to listen to her miseries. This time she was complaining that she had left a jumper at Bob's mother's house and it had not been returned.

'You'd think he could just wrap it up and post it to me,' she said in a voice that was definitely tending towards a whine. Maybe it was the voice that ended Sara's patience and made her explode with exasperation.

'For heaven's sake, Tabitha, don't be so stupid. I doubt if he has told his mother he has split up with you yet so she has probably just put it away to give to you next time she sees you.'

'But she's not going to see me,' wailed Tabitha.

'And whose fault is that? You broke your engagement. You told Bob you wanted nothing more to do with him. He has taken you at your word and it serves you right. Bob is a nice man and he loves his mother and is glad that she has found happiness with Sam. All you care about is what you want and your stupid wedding!'

With that she slammed the telephone down, only to spend the rest of the evening suffering from remorse. She had been cruel and unfair to her friend. How could she face her again?

She made her way slowly and unwillingly to work on Monday, hoping that she and Tabitha could avoid each other, but halfway through the morning her office door opened and Tabitha came in. Sara stood up, flustered and contrite.

'Tabitha, I'm so sorry about what I said! It wasn't fair of me.'

But Tabitha was smiling. 'You know perfectly well that you were right, and I'm here to thank you. Look!'

She held out her left hand. Her engagement ring was sparkling there, back in its usual place. Sara threw her arms joyously round her friend.

'Tabitha, I'm so glad! What happened?'

'Well, after you told me off I was furious. I fumed for an hour and then I began to think about what you said and I knew you were telling the truth. So before I could lose my nerve I called Bob and told him that I loved him and wanted us to be together again. He told me he'd been broken-hearted and so he came round immediately — and now we're back together again!'

'And do you agree about everything now?'

Tabitha's eyes slid away. 'We didn't discuss the wedding or Sam — we were just too busy telling each other how much we loved each other. I didn't want to spoil the moment.'

So there might still be trouble in the future, Sara thought, but contented herself by congratulating her friend on her regained happiness.

'Why don't the two of you come round to my place next Saturday?' she said impulsively. 'I will cook us a meal and we can celebrate your reunion.'

'I'd love that,' Tabitha accepted.

9

By Friday afternoon Sara had reluctantly decided that a happy Tabitha was nearly as exhausting as a miserable Tabitha. Each day she had to listen while Tabitha extolled Bob's virtues and told Sara how happy he made her while Sara smiled, nodded and wondered how long it was before she could escape back to work.

On Friday afternoon she went shopping for Saturday's meal instead of going straight home. Inside her own front door at last, Sara dumped the heavy bags on the kitchen table, rubbed her aching arms, and then poured herself a large glass of wine before sinking gratefully into an armchair and closing her eyes. Peace at last!

It would be nice to see Bob again, she told herself. She liked him, just as she liked Gordon, though she would never have fallen in love with either of them herself. Bob was dark and quiet, endlessly patient, while Gordon was fair-haired and exuberant, quick to anger but equally quickly pacified.

When she fell in love it would be with someone who knew his own mind and was polite but determined, like Walter; someone talented who worked hard, like Walter; someone who could confront violence fearlessly yet did not feel it unmanly to produce a good meal, like Walter; someone with hazel eyes and warm brown hair who could turn a bleak backyard into a garden, like Walter.

Sara sat up abruptly, her eyes wide, frantically considering what she had just been thinking, but could come to only one conclusion. She was in love with Walter! She lay back in her chair and groaned. She had fallen in love with a man who regarded her as a friend and preferred glamorous women like Nicola; a man who was now on the opposite side of the world for an indefinite length of time; a man who was achieving success and recognition which would probably take him far away from a mere secretary for the local council.

'I am a fool!' she told herself. 'I only think I am in love with Walter because I haven't met any other eligible young men for ages. I must get out more.' Shaken, she got up and poured herself another glass of wine. 'It's just as well he isn't here. What would I do, how would I behave if he and I were here together?'

At that moment she heard a key turn in the front door, and seconds later the living room door opened. Walter stood there, and Sara answered her own question by dropping her wine glass on the floor, taking three steps, and throwing her arms round his neck.

Walter rocked on his feet and then clasped her firmly to him and kissed her. The kiss went on for a long time and when it ended Walter and Sara looked at each other with mutual, happy bewilderment.

'What are you doing here?' Sara demanded. 'You are supposed to be in New York for weeks yet.'

'I came back because I couldn't bear to be away from you any longer,' Walter stated simply, and kissed her again. When he finally released her, he shook his head as if to clear it.

'We are just friends. You told me you didn't find me attractive.'

'I was lying,' Sara said firmly. 'Kiss me again.'

Finally they relaxed their hold on each other. 'Sara,' Walter breathed, 'I love you dearly, but I've been travelling for sixteen hours and I'm exhausted. Would you please pick your glass up, find another one, and pour me some wine?'

They ended up on the couch, smiling into each other's eyes.

'In my wildest dreams, and they have been pretty wild, I didn't expect this welcome home. I was wondering what I would do if I came in and found you here with George,' Walter said happily.

'George?' Sara said, frowning as she tried to remember who he was talking about. 'Oh, him! I think the police are looking for him.'

'Good!' said Walter emphatically.

'I did try and tell you about him but you didn't want to know. But what about Nicola? I met her and she told me what happened. Why did you tell her you didn't want to see her again?'

Walter shifted a little, looking uncomfortable. 'Well, I must admit that when she appeared at the party here I was bowled over. After all, she is very beautiful. When I asked her out to dinner I was definitely hoping that we could resume our relationship. But during the meal I realised she bored me. All she could talk about was herself and all the time I was longing to be back here with you.'

'Why didn't you tell me?'

'What could I say? I couldn't tell you that I had ditched a beautiful woman because I wanted you, because as far as I knew you weren't interested in me.'

Sara snuggled into his arms. 'And now you've come back to me, rich and successful. I've heard about the panda money.'

She felt him laugh silently. 'It's a nice windfall, though it doesn't exactly make me rich. I've still got to go back to New York to finish what I was doing.' He sat up, displacing her. 'Incidentally, I'd better ring Gordon. I'll have to get together with him soon. Move over, I'll be back soon.'

He heaved himself reluctantly off the couch and soon she could hear his voice as he explained to Gordon where he was. Then there was a silence as he listened to Gordon, and then she heard him again.

'You have? That's great! Why don't the two of you come over here tomorrow and you can tell us all about it?'

He came back smiling to sink down on the couch again. 'Elaine and Gordon have found a house, so they are going to tell us all about it and show us the photographs.'

'I'm glad for them,' Sara said, and then tensed, remembering. 'But Tabitha and Bob are coming here for a meal tomorrow.'

'We'll just add a few more potatoes.'

'You don't understand!' She told him about Tabitha and Bob's recent parting and reconciliation. 'Seeing another couple who can afford a house of their own may upset them.'

'That's their problem,' Walter said firmly. 'Now, I'm going to kiss you again and then I must have something to eat!'

Sara woke the next day to a world transformed. She loved and was loved.

'Shall we tell the others?' she asked Walter over breakfast and he laughed.

'I doubt if we will need to tell them. From the moment she met you Elaine kept telling me that you and I would end up together, and I suspect Tabitha thought the same.'

Tabitha and Bob were the first to arrive that afternoon. Sara took advantage of a discussion between Bob and

Walter to draw Tabitha aside and tell her the news. Her friend gasped with delight and then congratulated her warmly.

'Bob thought you were made for each other, but I thought you had fallen for George Sayers. I'm glad you've chosen Walter, however. He's much nicer.' Her voice became wistful. 'And you haven't got to worry about where to live, either.'

Before Sara could reply Bob appeared and hugged her.

'Walter has told me the good news.'

Behind him Walter was holding a bottle of champagne and glasses.

'And now we can all drink a toast.' He ceremonially opened the bottle, filled the glasses and passed them to the others before he held his own aloft. 'To love and happiness!'

A knock on the door signalled the arrival of Gordon and Elaine, and soon they were also congratulating Sara and Walter and toasting them with champagne.

Then Elaine took a sheaf of papers from her handbag.

'Look! This is the house we are going to buy!' She spread out the printed sheets on the table. 'It is a three-bedroomed semi, and it has got a largish garden as well as a garage.'

'When are you moving?'

'In six weeks. The couple who own it are moving to an apartment in Spain, and we haven't got to sell anything, so it is going to be a quick and simple transaction.' Elaine smoothed out a photograph lovingly. 'I'm looking forward to it so much, although in a way I will miss our flat. We have been very happy there.'

'It is a nice flat,' Walter agreed, and added casually, 'It's a pity Tabitha and Bob can't take it over.'

There was silence. Sara was taken aback by Walter's lack of tact and glared at him but he was looking at Tabitha, and finally the silence was broken by Tabitha saying in an uncertain voice, 'Why can't we?'

Gordon shrugged.

'Well, I understand that you and Bob

are not getting married till next year. You would have to pay the rent from the moment we leave, and the landlord would want a large deposit anyway.'

'I'm afraid we can't afford it,' Bob said despondently, and then Tabitha swung round to face him, gripping his arms.

'Yes we can!'

'We've got the money we have saved for the wedding! That would pay the deposit.'

'But what about the rent?'

Tabitha smiled triumphantly. 'We can get married within six weeks and move in as soon as Elaine and Gordon leave.'

Bob stared at her incredulously. 'But what about the wedding, the big wedding you want so much?'

Tabitha managed a smile. 'For a week I thought I'd lost you. I realised then that being married to you is far more important than spending a fortune on an elaborate wedding. Your mother is getting married quickly and quietly and so could we.'

Bob's face lit up. 'If you mean it, it will solve so many problems. Are you sure, really sure?'

'I am really sure,' Tabitha told him firmly.

'I think I'll open some more champagne,' Walter announced.

Elaine started to give details of the flat but was interrupted by Gordon.

'Why don't we drive you over and show it to you? The landlord lives in the ground floor flat so you can speak to him about the tenancy. We'll recommend you.'

The idea was approved, and while Gordon telephoned the landlord and arranged for them all to see him, Sara managed to draw Tabitha aside.

'Shouldn't you think about this, Tabitha? It does mean giving up your dream of the perfect wedding, and I know how much that meant to you.'

Tabitha smiled. 'I know, and there will be times when I regret losing that dream. But if I have to choose between life with Bob in our own home and a big wedding, then I'll choose Bob and home.'

Sara agreed to go along with the two couples but Walter shook his head.

'I've spent a lot of time travelling recently,' he said firmly.

'I'm going to stay here and have a rest.'

Once at the flat there was an enjoyable session of inspecting facilities, checking storage space and exclaiming at the décor, which featured some of Gordon's fantasy figures, before Bob, Tabitha and Gordon went to see the landlord. They were back within half an hour, all smiles.

'I think he was relieved that he didn't have to go through a lot of fuss reletting the flat,' Bob said happily. 'Anyway, it will be ours in six weeks.' He hugged Tabitha. 'Now we've just got to get our wedding arranged.'

'I insist on a pretty dress,' Tabitha said, and Elaine laughed triumphantly.

'Tabitha, that won't be a problem. Gordon and I know a costume designer who owes us a favour. She'll make you a fabulous frock.'

Conversation about the flat and the dress were obviously going to go on for some time, and Sara wanted to get back to Walter, so a taxi was called to take her home.

Back at the house, far from resting quietly Walter was crawling about the kitchen floor with a measuring tape. He stood up as Sara came in, brushing the knees of his jeans.

'Did everything go all right?'

'They've practically signed the contract! But what are you doing?'

He waved an arm at the kitchen. 'I thought we could use the money I've received to refit the kitchen and bathroom. I was just trying to see if we could fit in a dishwasher.'

Sara shook her head. 'Walter, you can't spend a lot of money on my house.'

He looked at her sharply. 'Your house? I was thinking of it as our house. After all, when we are married . . . '

Sara interrupted him. 'When we are married?'

He looked at her uncertainly. 'Well, we are going to get married, aren't we?'

Sara gladly abandoned any visions of a romantic proposal. 'Of course we are!'

The measuring tape was forgotten in favour of embracing Sara, but after a while she pushed Walter away and sniffed.

'Can you smell something burning?'

Walter dived for the oven and opened the door. Smoke billowed out. It was the meal for six which had been going to be served that evening.

'It's ruined,' Walter said gloomily, and then cheered up. 'Never mind. If the others do reappear we can send out for pizzas. Meanwhile, let's see if there is any champagne left.'

There was enough and they sank down on the couch to enjoy the pleasure of being together and knowing they loved each other.

'Tabitha and Bob are planning to get married seven weeks from today,' Sara said dreamily.

'Seven weeks?' Walter frowned. 'We may not be back.'

'Back? Back from where?'

'From our honeymoon in New York. I have to go back there within three weeks, but if we go to the registry office on Monday to fill in the necessary forms we can get married fifteen days later and I can take you with me when I go back to New York. You said the other day that you had some holiday due.'

Sara was sitting upright, spluttering champagne. 'But we can't get married so soon! You haven't even met my parents!'

'Ah. Well, it so happens that your mother called while you were out. We had a good long talk and she's coming down next weekend with your father to meet me and plan the wedding.'

Sara was waving her hands, making incoherent noises.

'What's the matter, Sara? You said you wanted to marry me.'

Sara nodded.

'Don't you want to marry me soon?'

Sara nodded again.

'Would you like to go somewhere else for our honeymoon?'

Sara shook her head, searching for the words to explain that she felt as if she were being swept away by a mountain torrent and needed time to grasp the information that was swamping her.

Walter's face cleared.

'I know what's the matter. There's no need to worry. Mrs Drew has agreed to water the plants.'

THE END

We do hope that you have enjoyed reading this large print book.

Did you know that all of our titles are available for purchase?

We publish a wide range of high quality large print books including:
Romances, Mysteries, Classics
General Fiction
Non Fiction and Westerns

Special interest titles available in large print are:
The Little Oxford Dictionary
Music Book, Song Book
Hymn Book, Service Book

Also available from us courtesy of Oxford University Press:
Young Readers' Dictionary
(large print edition)
Young Readers' Thesaurus
(large print edition)

For further information or a free brochure, please contact us at:
Ulverscroft Large Print Books Ltd.,
The Green, Bradgate Road, Anstey,
Leicester, LE7 7FU, England.
Tel: (00 44) **0116 236 4325**
Fax: (00 44) **0116 234 0205**